TALES OF PANGLORIA

Book One

BARNEY'S BEDSTEAD

Graham Peebles

Front cover artwork and interior maps by Graham Peebles.
Front cover photographic images courtesy of Shutterstock.com

ISBN-13: 978-1503230729
ISBN-10: 1503230724

ABOUT THE AUTHOR

Graham Peebles is an author who hails from the Black Country, deep in the heart of the West Midlands, England.

Having retired from teaching in 2013 he decided to pursue other activities, in particular a lifelong ambition to write a series of fantasy adventure novels for older children and young at heart adults. Having made a conscious decision to publish independently, Graham has joined the proud ranks of independent, ethical authors.

Graham enjoys performing with a blues based rock band and also likes to draw and paint with various local art groups. He currently lives with his beloved wife of forty years or so, his daughter and two cats, plus an ever growing collection of guitars, much to the annoyance of his wife!

Visit his website: *grahampeeblesauthor.com*

For Yvonne and Louise, for believing…
Edna and Jane for reading and good advice…

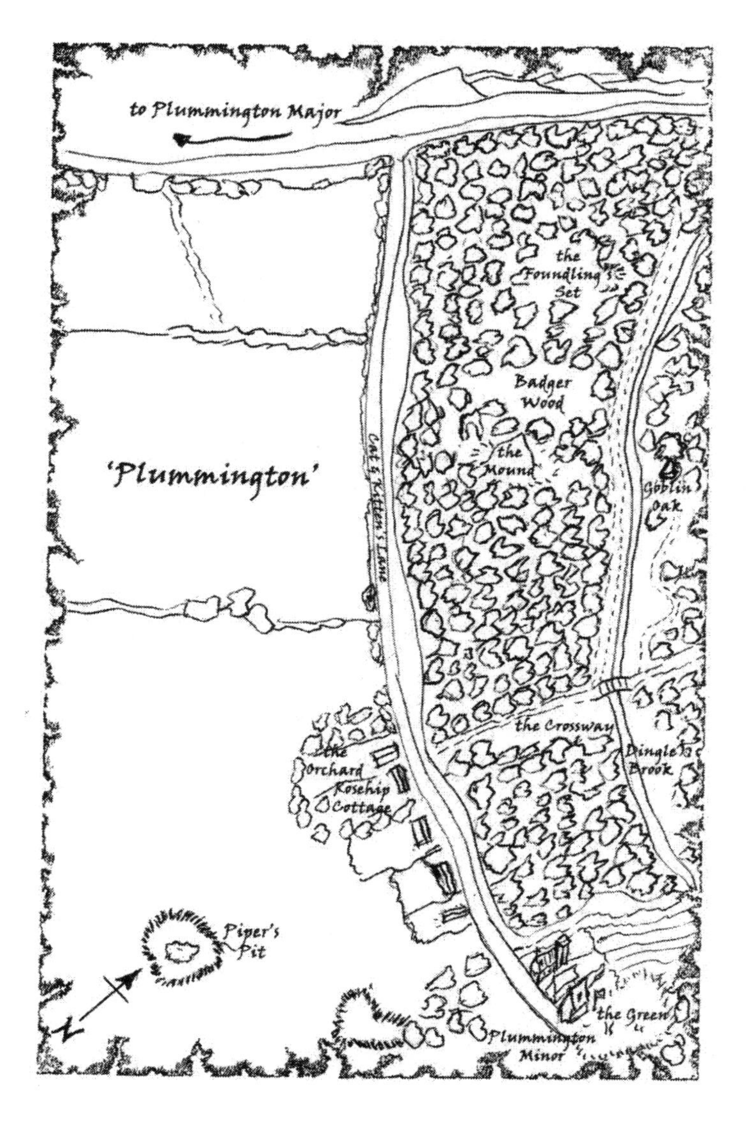
to Plummington Major
'Plummington'
the Foundling's Set
Badger Wood
the Mound
Goblin Oak
Cat & Kitten's Lane
the Crossway
Dingle Brook
the Orchard
Rosehip Cottage
Piper's Pit
the Green
Plummington Minor
N

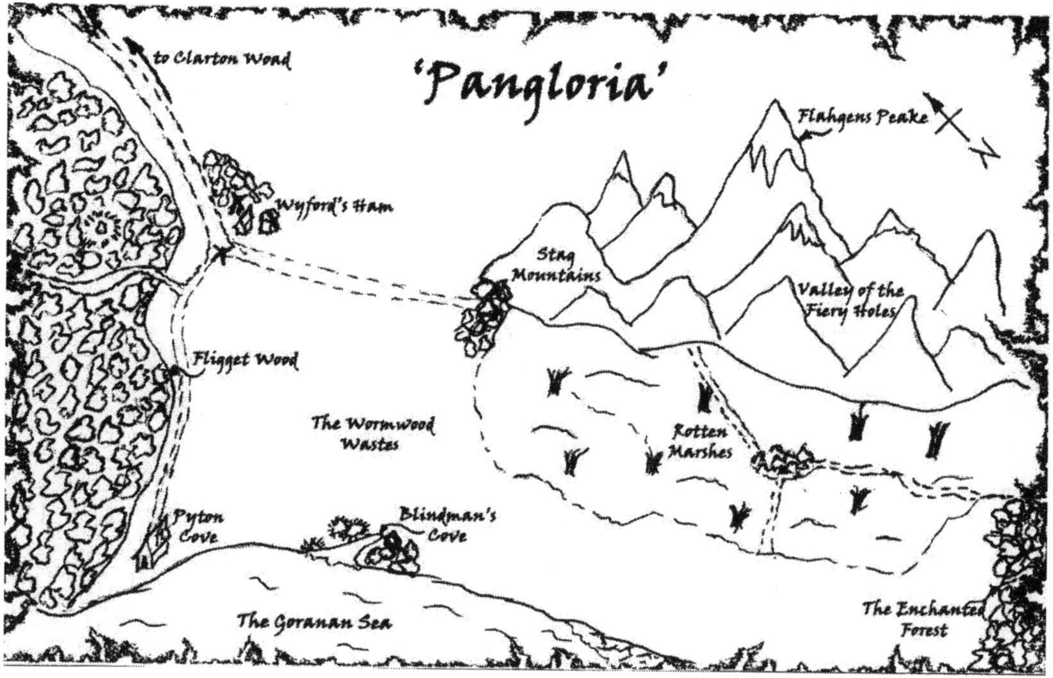

'Pangloria'
to Clarton Wood
Wyford's Ham
Flahgens Peake
N
Stag Mountains
Valley of the Fiery Holes
Fligget Wood
The Wormwood Wastes
Rotten Marshes
Pyton Cove
Blindman's Cove
The Goranan Sea
The Enchanted Forest

TALES OF PANGLORIA

Book One

BARNEY'S BEDSTEAD

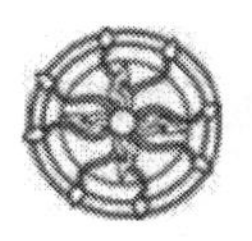

CONTENTS

~ CHAPTER ONE ~

Bumps and Strange Doings

The figure of an old man stood before the gigantic rock face of Flahgens Peake, studying its hard glassy surface with interest. He pulled his travel stained forest green cloak tightly about his slender body and carefully looked around him in the darkness to make certain that he was alone. The wind was howling like a pack of wolves as the notorious weather of the Stag Mountains closed in around him. Feeling the wind's chill, he pulled his damp cloak even tighter.

As he stared up at the dark, brooding sky, Rookwort mumbled to himself, 'It's going to rain again soon. I suppose I'd better get on with it.' And with a sigh he began the preparations for casting the spell which would enable him to enter the face of the mountain that stood before him.

It was rumoured in Pangloria that Flahgens Peake was a magic portal into another world and made by the nature goddess, known simply as the Damsel. It was also rumoured that deep within the heart of the mountain were riches and magical artefacts beyond anyone's wildest dreams. These were what Rookwort had come to find. The old man was well known across Pangloria, but was something of an odd character, even in this strange parallel world.

Rookwort had a reputation for being something of a bungling wizard, on account of his rather poor attempts at performing magic.

He did occasionally get the odd spell right, mind you; but mostly when Rookwort performed some spell or complex charm, they tended to have an unfortunate effect upon whomever or whatever the spell was aimed at!

Because of these botched attempts at magic, Rookwort had ended up being treated like someone who'd contracted a nasty, contagious disease and as a result, people now tended to avoid him. This had left Rookwort feeling angry and deeply mistrustful of others, not to mention that he was now thoroughly fed up with being the object of people's cruel jokes. But this time, he was going to show them all!

Rookwort had listened to the stories about the treasures of Flahgens Peake and had dreamed of finding them for some time. And all that he needed to do now was gain entrance into the mountain, find the rare spell books of legend, and then he would show everyone what a real wizard could do.

The strangest thing about all of this was that Rookwort *did* have the ability to perform innate magic. But his problem was that he had never been able to realise this!

All Rookwort needed to do was search within himself, and he would find that he was more than capable of wielding very powerful magic. It was simply a case of self-belief. His older brother had always told him, when they were children, 'You can do it, you know, Rook. You've just got to keep on trying, it'll come, you'll see.'

Bah! It was alright for him to say that, thought Rookwort gloomily; everything always came very easily to you, brother – and now to cap it all you went and left me on my own, to live with those detestable folk who inhabit that other world. Some help you've been, huh!

Rookwort went through the necessary mental exercises in order to calm his mind and focus his thoughts upon the casting of this important spell. When his preparations were complete, he straightened his body and began to force his will upon the dark face of the mountain.

After several long minutes of total concentration, he spread his arms out wide, and with his palms facing forward began to recite the words of the complex incantation that would open the portal within the side of the mountain.

His voice, now rising to a crescendo, boomed loudly as he uttered the final word of power, 'Accessienta!' Rookwort then nodded his head submissively and waited.

Feeling exhausted, he held his breath in quiet anticipation, remaining totally still. For what seemed like an eternity, nothing appeared to happen. Then, without any warning, a flash of silver light lit up the darkness, and for a split second, a long, narrow opening appeared within the face of the mountain.

Rookwort could have sworn that he had glimpsed a dark shadowy figure of someone moving within the centre of the opening. He caught the foul stench of something that was rotting!

He shook his head, wondering what it was that he had seen, and when Rookwort looked up once more his excitement disappeared in an instant. He saw that the face of the mountain had remained totally untouched and looked as unforgiving as ever.

He almost tripped as he ran forward and began to panic as he examined the surface of the mountain. His hands searched desperately as they flew over its hard contours, looking for signs of the opening that he had seen a few moments earlier. Rookwort gasped in disappointment as he finally realised that the spell hadn't had any effect whatsoever upon the mountain!

'Failed again!' He spat out the words with a venomous hiss, and finally, losing all self-control, proceeded to stomp around in a rage, totally disgusted at his pathetic attempt.

After calling himself things like 'stupid' and 'worthless', he managed to finally calm himself down, and shrugged his narrow shoulders in final resignation of yet another failure.

Then with a heavy sigh and an even heavier heart, Rookwort began the long, lonely trudge back down into the valley below.

'I could have sworn I'd done it this time,' he mumbled to himself bitterly as he headed down towards the Rotten Marshes. Pulling his cloak tightly around his chilled body once more, he trudged on despondently, as the cruel mountain mist began to close in around him.

As he slowly stumbled along the narrow path, several pairs of unfriendly eyes followed his progress, laughing with an evil hiss as he disappeared from sight. The wicked creatures returned to their vigil, each eagerly watching the gateway within the mountain, waiting with greedy anticipation for the return of their brethren and the precious cargo that it had gone to steal.

Meanwhile, deep within the heart of Badger Wood, the Foundling lay curled up, warm and fast asleep in its soft bedding of moss and leaves. It had the appearance of a tiny badger cub, except that its fur was pure white in colour, and it only had faint dark stripes of a badger running down the length of its long, gentle face. The Foundling's nose, paws and eyes were a vivid pink colour, giving her the tell-tale features of an albino, making it quite obvious that she was a very special creature.

The Foundling had been born out of the Earth's natural magic, and she had always been a living talisman. As such, she had been sent by the Damsel to protect the creatures of Badger Wood from the ravages of mankind. The Foundling had lived out her normal lifespan, as would any other wild creature, but she had always been reborn, sometimes as a fox, a hare, a deer, or a bird, in fact whatever wild creature that the Damsel herself had chosen.

The Foundling's one purpose was to protect the wild creatures of Badger Wood, which it did of course by its very existence. The fact that it was imbibed with very powerful Earth magic ensured the protection of this earthly haven. There are two things that a Foundling can be identified by, one is that it is always female, and secondly, that its colour is always pure white.

As the Foundling remained in a deep slumber, oblivious to her surroundings and the soft nightly noises Badger Wood, her parents and siblings were foraging for the food that they would bring back to share with the tiny white cub. The badger cub was so deep within her world of sleep that she was quite unaware of the dark pair of hands that lifted her body stealthily from her comfortable leafy bedding!

As the first light of dawn appeared on the horizon, the small family of badgers returned to their sett, and were chattering excitedly and playfully as they jumped and tumbled over one another.

After playing for a while they entered the badger sett, quietly so as to avoid waking the Foundling. As they came to the deepest part of the sett, they snuffled around the soft bedding, following the Foundling's scent, only to find that she wasn't there! In a panic they ran around, frantically searching inside and outside of the sett for the missing badger cub, their cries alerting the other animals within wood.

The badgers' desperate calls travelled like wildfire through Badger Wood, and soon every creature both large and small began to search for the missing Foundling, but she had disappeared without a trace. In that moment they suddenly realised that she had been taken! Within a short time a great pall of sadness and fear descended upon Badger Wood, and in the early morning air came a haunting, pitiful sound from within its depths – the animals were crying!

Barney Betts lay slumped over his desk, and was hardly aware of the piece of blackboard chalk that had just bounced off his head. It was only the roar of his teacher's voice that brought him wide awake, as he was suddenly jolted out of his stupor.

'Barnaby Betts! What on earth do you think you are doing? How *dare* you fall asleep in my lesson – again! This is the third time this week – you're obviously *not* going to bed at a respectable hour for children, are you? Well, my lad, I'm going to be having a word with your mother about this. Now sit up straight, and *concentrate*.'

Barney's teacher, Miss Holfirth, paused to let the fury of her words sink in. 'You will see me after class for punishment and heaven help you if I catch you asleep in my lesson again. Now sit up!'

Still angry, the teacher, Miss Agnes Holfirth, stomped across the classroom to a very large blackboard and continued with her arithmetic lesson.

Agnes Holfirth was a middle-aged spinster and had been teaching at Plummington Major junior school for the last thirty years. Tall, slim and sprightly, she was a very attractive woman, regarded as a good catch by most of the eligible men in the Plummington area. Therefore, it was considered more than a little odd by the inhabitants of Plummington that Agnes had never wanted to get married, and she had never been seen walking out with a man.

'That's because she's a sour-faced old bat!' was often the comment given by pupils who had recently incurred her displeasure, and given the way Agnes Holfirth dealt with miscreant pupils or unconcerned parents, she had gained the reputation of being a person that one did not cross – or fall out with.

Here we go again, thought Barney, more blinking lines I suppose. He tried desperately to cover up another yawn with the palm of his hand and at the same time avoid his teacher's angry stare.

Barney Betts was an eleven-year-old boy, going on twelve, with a freckly face and a head of sandy coloured hair, which very rarely came into contact with the teeth of a comb! And only then when his mother became so fed up with her son's raggle-taggle mop that she would tug and pull at his unruly hair in an attempt to keep Barney looking reasonably tidy!

Despite his wayward appearance, Barney was quite

popular with almost everyone who lived in and around Plummington. Most folk called him Barney, except Miss Holfirth of course, who always insisted on calling her pupils by their 'correct' name.

Even Barney's mum only ever called him Barnaby when she was telling him off, and that seemed to be almost every day just lately. Barney wasn't very big for his age; he wasn't skinny like Freddie Puckworth, for example, or chunky like Beefy Rowley. In fact, Barney was just a normal sort of boy. Mind you, he could run faster than anyone else in his class and was more than a fair footballer, although cricket was really his favourite game – he had played for the school eleven for the last two seasons.

Barney's other passion was shooting his homemade catapult at old tin cans or other targets with his best friends Lenny and Lorna Barker, known locally as the Barker twins. The three children were all crack shots, particularly Lenny who, it was reputed, could shoot a boil off your nose without breaking the skin!

So it was fairly plain to see that Barney Betts was nothing more than an ordinary eleven-year-old boy with unruly hair, a freckly face which always seemed to bear an impish expression and the scabby knees of someone who enjoyed the rough and tumble of the school playground.

The fact that Barney had been walking around in a daze, seemed to have gone unnoticed by everyone in his class. He hadn't been sleeping very well for the last few nights, mainly due to his single bed being broken. It had to be propped up on a rickety old wooden box that he had found lying around in his dad's old shed.

Using your bed for a trampoline isn't really a good idea, and that's exactly what Barney had done four nights earlier.

It had been in the middle of the night when Barney's house had been shaken by the sound of a very loud bump! Barney had got up to use the chamber pot under his bed, as his house only had one toilet and that was outside at the end of the coalhouse!

Barney just couldn't be bothered going out into the cold night air to use the lavatory late at night. Besides, he never knew what might be lurking in there; maybe a dirty great rat, or worse still, a ghost!

As he jumped back into his nice warm bed, he felt it collapse with a loud bang! He looked down and saw that the end of his bed lay in a broken heap upon the bedroom floor. 'Oh crikey,' Barney muttered in a panic, 'how the heck did that happen?'

Suddenly, he heard a loud shriek from his mother's bedroom which was situated right next to his. 'Barnaby Betts! What on earth have you done?'

Barney then heard a noise which sounded like an express train thundering along the landing and his mother burst through his bedroom door with a loud crash!

Barney's mum stood framed in the doorway with her hair curlers sticking out all over her head. She was wearing her plum coloured dressing gown and sporting an old pair of mauve mule-type slippers. 'What are you trying to do, Barney, demolish the house?' she said crossly. 'I know it's not much, but we *do* happen to live here.'

Suddenly her eyes grew wide as they came to rest on the wreckage that was once Barney's bed. With a gasp she cried, 'Oh Barney, look what you've done!' Then letting out a heavy sigh, she slumped down onto Barney's bedside stool. 'There's no way that we can repair that bed, and goodness knows how I'm going to afford a new one,' she cried in desperation. 'It's taken me three months just save enough for a new pair of school shoes for you and now this.' She gestured towards the broken bed. 'I just don't know what I'm going to do.'

Barney suddenly felt very awkward and really sorry for his mum. Olivia Betts had brought Barney up, her only child, on her own, ever since Barney's father had died.

Her husband Ralph had been an RAF pilot who had been killed at the very end of the Second World War. Rationing had only recently ended and some household items were still scarce and could be rather expensive, which left poor Olivia very little money for more expensive purchases such as new beds!

Ralph had died leaving Olivia and Barney virtually un-provided for. The house that they lived in was a small old cottage, which Olivia had rented, and was situated at number two Cat and Kittens Lane, in Plummington Minor.

The landlord of their home was a kindly old man named George Hopwood, who always tried to help the Betts family whenever he could. He limped rather badly on account of an old war wound he had picked up somewhere in the African desert, so as a result he had a fair bit of sympathy for the Betts family. The fact that George Hopwood had more than a soft spot for Olivia Betts was common knowledge in Plummington Minor, which being a small village that absolutely thrived on local gossip, had at times caused her some embarrassment.

Barney stared back at his mum sadly and replied in a very small voice, 'I'm ever so sorry, Mum, but it was an accident, it just sort of collapsed when I got back into bed.'

Olivia gazed at her son. Feeling sorry for the hurt look upon his face and with a supreme effort she said, 'Well, Barney, there's nothing for it, you'll just have to go down to Dad's old shed and bring his toolbox to prop up your bed, just for now, and I'll see what they have in that old junk shop in Plummington Major on Saturday.'

Her face became a little sterner once more as, wagging her finger, she scolded, 'You'd better pray that they have something there, my lad, or it's going to be a little bit uncomfortable for a while. Now, off you go and find that box. I'm going back to bed to get some sleep because it looks like I'm going to need it. I'll just have to do some extra cleaning, because new beds do not pay for themselves!' Standing up slowly she added, 'Well goodnight, dear, and don't forget to lock the back door will you? And *please*, don't break anything else.'

Olivia made her way wearily out of the bedroom, leaving him standing there feeling quite ashamed and sorry for himself. 'Oh, I really hate being poor!' he mumbled under his breath.

Barney was still thinking about his mum when he looked up to see the blonde-haired heads of his two best friends, the Barker twins, staring at him, along with the rest of the class.

Lorna Barker had a 'I knew you'd get caught again' expression on her face, and her twin brother Lenny simply gave him a rueful grin. Barney was very tempted to bob out his tongue in a rude gesture, but thought better of it. He didn't want to incur the wrath of Miss Holfirth again. She was well known for her no nonsense approach to pupils and could be an absolute terror to any pupil who didn't follow her rules in class!

Miss Holfirth's commanding voice rang out once more, 'Now with Barnaby Betts' permission, *perhaps* we can continue to study the number problems upon the blackboard.' With a scathing look at Barney, Miss Holfirth continued with the lesson, despite the heavy sigh that came from the rest of the class.

'Huh! I really hate arithmetic,' sighed Barney under his breath. 'Rotten load of old rubbish.' And with another heavy sigh he put his head down and began to write.

'I mean, it's just not *fair*, is it?' Barney groaned. 'Two hundred lines *and* I've got to hand them in by tomorrow morning! My mum's going to half kill me. I reckon that Miss Holfirth's really got it in for me.' Feeling a deep sense of injustice and his face starting to go red with rage, he added, 'I only dozed off for a few seconds.'

'Well, you shouldn't have got caught then, should you?' replied the teasing but knowing voice of Lorna Barker, who was smiling, just a little mischievously, as they made their way home from school. 'You never see *me* getting caught, do you?'

'Oh, ha-ha, hark at little miss perfect, always sucking up to the teacher. Do you know what? She's going to cotton on to you one of these days, miss clever clogs! And when she does, I hope she really gives you what for,' said Lenny. 'Mind you, Barney, I think you were dead lucky not to get caned – after all, it's the third time this week that she's caught you dropping off to sleep.'

'Well, I can't help it, can I?' Barney whined. 'My bed's all broken – I bounced on it a bit and it just sort of collapsed. It's propped up on an old wooden toolbox of my dad's, which is okay, until I move in my sleep. Now I'm awake most of the night because I'm frightened of waking up my mum. I don't know, maybe Miss Holfirth just hates me.'

'Oh no,' Lorna announced rather smugly, her blue eyes twinkling in amusement. 'I don't think that she just hates *you*, Barney. She hates all boys. But who wouldn't when they're all as dim as you two, I mean, really!' she added with a laugh.

'Oh put a sock in it!' shouted Barney and Lenny, and they began to chase after Lorna as she ran away still teasing the two boys.

Laughing and joking, they began to stroll more leisurely along the road from Plummington Major. They took the usual right turn into Cat and Kittens Lane, which was typical of the leafy country lanes of southern England. The lane ran alongside the edge of Badger Wood and led down a gentle slope into the small village of Plummington Minor. As the children continued their journey home, they breathed deeply as they took in the scent of honeysuckle and wild herbs which grew among the hedgerows, while revelling in the warmth of the summer sun upon their backs.

They stopped suddenly. Several cries and howls came from the depth of the trees within Badger Wood. Lenny stood quite still and with an expression of concern on his face said, 'Listen to that lot, it's usually pretty quiet in there, it always seems a bit strange, but it's never been this noisy.'

As the three children continued listening to the sounds from within the wood, Lorna spoke almost with a whisper, 'Well it's not very quiet now is it? It's almost as if everything's been disturbed; hark at those cries; it sounds as if every creature in the wood is upset. No – something's definitely, not right!'

'Well my mum's always saying that there have been strange doings in that wood for years,' replied Barney, with an awestruck expression. 'She reckons it's haunted!'

'I wouldn't nod off in there then, if I were you,' warned Lenny, giving his friend a mocking smile. 'You might just get lost and disappear for ever!'

Roaring with laughter at Lenny's jest, the children carried on walking down the lane towards home.

None of them noticed that a pair of inquisitive jet black eyes was watching them carefully, from within the trees!

They came at last to the familiar white gate that led into the garden of Rosehip Cottage, a quaint little thatched dwelling with clean white walls and a neatly laid out vegetable garden.

Rosehip Cottage had been home to Lorna and Lenny ever since they had been born. Their father Basil was the well-respected manager of Theakstones Bank, located in Plummington Major, while their mother Rose stayed at home looking after her beloved little cottage, her husband and the twins, whom she doted upon.

It was a well-known fact in Plummington Minor that the Barker family, although not rich, were comfortably well off.

The Barker twins had always been the best of friends with Barney, ever since they had been tiny toddlers, and as they had always been happy in each other's company and only lived within a couple of hundred yards of each other, they naturally became firm friends.

As the twins went to walk through the garden gate

they heard a loud rustling from the undergrowth at the side of the path leading down towards the entrance into Badger Wood. The children were looking and listening for the cause of the rustling, when suddenly from out of the undergrowth there emerged a large grey dog that came bounding towards them on four huge paws.

The dog had the look of a large grey timber wolf, and was wagging his tail excitedly as he let out a deep throaty bark causing the children to jump and squeal with delight.

'Bouncer!' cried Lorna. 'Where *have* you been? Chasing rabbits again, I suppose,' she said as she scratched behind the dog's ears briskly with her fingers.

'Yeah, more likely been up to no good, I'll bet,' Lenny added with a grin as Bouncer jumped up and placed both of his front paws on Barney's shoulders. Barney almost collapsed under the weight of the large dog. Bouncer's tongue gave his face a great slurping lick.

'Oh *don't* let him do that, my dear,' said Mrs Barker, who had come into the garden to investigate the commotion outside her cottage. 'It's not very hygienic to have Bouncer licking your face like that you know, especially when you don't know where he's been, and heaven knows where that is. Eh, you rogue,' she added, smiling at Bouncer, who was now running around the children, barking happily.

As she turned to walk back into her homely little cottage, she said to the twins, 'Tea in ten minutes, my dears, fresh scones, with strawberry jam and cream. And I've just baked a lovely fruit cake. Would you like to stay for tea, Barney?' she asked with a kind smile.

Barney was sorely tempted to accept the offer of such a scrumptious tea, but shook his head and replied,

'I'd really love to, Mrs Barker, honestly, but I've got loads to do and Mum's expecting me home for my tea.'

'Barney's got lines again from Miss Holfirth, Mum,' said Lorna, looking reproachfully at Barney.

'What on earth for?' exclaimed Mrs Barker with a frown. 'I know that Agnes can be a little hard at times, but just before your summer holidays is a bit *too* hard if you ask me!' She shook her head and with a sigh added, 'Well, off you go and get them done, my dear. The sooner it's done, the sooner it's out of the way, that's what I always say.'

Barney nodded reluctantly, feeling wretched at missing out on one of Mrs Barker's splendid teas. 'Oh! And Barney, pass on my regards to your mum.' Then with a wave of her hand, she disappeared back into the cottage.

'Fancy a game of cricket later, Barney?' Lenny asked with a smile. 'It's going to be a nice evening, and we really could do with the practise, you know.'

'Be great if I could,' Barney replied, miserably. 'But I've got to hand in those lines tomorrow, *remember*?'

'Ah,' muttered Lenny thoughtfully. 'I'd forgotten that she'd given you two hundred to do. Oh well, not to worry,' he added with a sigh. 'I guess that I'll just have to resort to my ever trusty back up, wont I, Lorna? Except that girls just can't *bowl*, even if their lives depended on it.'

Lenny suddenly winced as a sharp blow hit him squarely on his arm. 'Ouch! That really hurt,' he scowled at Lorna, as he rubbed his arm, which he discovered, was rapidly going numb!

'Wow! Good punch, Lorna,' said Barney giving her a pat on the back. 'He really asked for that.'

Lorna walked away with her nose in the air and a

self-satisfied grin etched on her face. She mumbled something that sounded like, 'Boys! Hah!'

Barney simply shook his head and turned for home. As he walked away he shouted to Lenny, 'See you tomorrow then,' and with a wave of his hand he ran the last few yards towards home and an evening of two hundred lines for Miss Holfirth.

Neither Barney nor the twins were aware of the mysterious little figure that had been hiding and watching them from the undergrowth of Badger Wood. The keen, jet black eyes followed Barney all of the way to the front door of his home, before the strangely clad little figure stepped back into the trees and vanished.

~ CHAPTER TWO ~

Crumpshaw's Emporium

The next morning, as Barney handed in his blotted pages of lines to Miss Holfirth, she gave him a stern look as she scolded him, 'It was for your own good, you know; perhaps this will teach you to stay awake in future.' Taking a deep breath, she added, 'Now I've had a little chat with your mother, Barnaby, and she told me about your mishap with the bed. Why didn't *you* tell me?'

Barney felt his face beginning to colour up and he started to stammer. 'But… but.'

'Well, never mind,' replied Miss Holfirth, and she continued to speak before Barney could say anything else. 'I hear that you and your mum are going to look for a replacement in Plummington Major tomorrow. So *you* just make sure that you look after it, young man, or you'll have *me* to answer to. Now, go back to your desk and carry on with your essay.'

'Yes, Miss,' Barney mumbled in reply, glad to be off the hook once again.

The rest of the week whizzed by without incident, and before they knew it, Friday had arrived. Everyone looked forward to Fridays, but today was extra special, mainly because it was the last day of the school year and the beginning of the summer holidays.

Unusually, Miss Holfirth relented and allowed her pupils to play board games in class instead of the usual arithmetic, geography or spelling lessons, and as a result everyone was happy and filled with excitement at the thought of six whole weeks without school.

As Barney and the twins made their way home that afternoon, they began to talk about some of the things which they could do in the coming six weeks holiday.

'I'm not sure that we'll be going away to the seaside this summer,' said Lenny glumly. 'Mum told me that Dad's going to be really busy at the bank during the next few weeks and that we may have to wait until the autumn half term to go away on holiday. It must be really awful to have to go to work all of the time,' he added shaking his head.

'Oh, I've never been on holiday, or even seen the sea,' Barney replied miserably. 'What with Mum earning so little, we just can't afford it. But my mum says what you've never had you never miss – still, it would be great to go on holiday, wouldn't it?'

He suddenly felt Lorna place a gentle hand upon his shoulder, and very quietly she said, 'Never mind, Barney, maybe your mum will let you come with us on holiday during the next half term.'

'Hey, wouldn't that be great!' exclaimed Lenny excitedly. 'We'll ask our dad, I'm sure he'll agree.'

Barney suddenly felt very self-conscious, but he also felt a nice warm glow inside him. It's really good to have friends who care, he thought, as he began to blush. He broke into a sudden run as he headed down the lane to hide his embarrassment, shouting to the twins, 'Come on then, you two. I'll race you back home; the last one there is dope!'

Taking up the challenge, the twins and Barney sprinted down the lane and out of sight of the jet black eyes that had been watching them, once more, from the dark shadows of Badger Wood. As the children drew closer to the lime-washed walls of Rosehip Cottage, Lenny stopped suddenly and hissed, 'Hey you two, look over there!' He nodded in the direction of the path leading into the wood.

They looked across to the path and saw the familiar figure of Jed Hopwood heading towards the Crossway. This was a small dirt track that led to the bridge spanning Dingle Brook, a narrow but deep watercourse that snaked its way through Badger Wood. Jed was sneaking stealthily along the track, as if he didn't want anyone to see him.

Barney noticed that he was carrying a double-barrelled shotgun in his hands and a large canvas bag on his shoulder. 'I wonder what *he's* getting up to,' Lorna snorted. 'What a horrible man. Do you know that he shot Daphne Curtis's cat last week, and it had to be put to sleep. All he did was smile and say that the gun went off by accident! He didn't even bother to say that he was sorry, the cruel beast.'

'That's not all,' Barney added. 'Jed's just a big bully, and he's always picking on little kids. He twisted Billy Goode's arm the other day and only because Billy's football bounced and hit him on the leg!'

'Yeah, I heard that too,' replied Lenny. 'Kids are about *all* that he can handle. Mind you, if Billy's dad catches hold of him, he'll give him a bloody nose, *and* it'll serve him right.'

At that moment Bouncer ran up to the three children and started nuzzling his head up against them as his tail wagged furiously. Barney turned to the twins and said, 'How do fancy going over to the village green after tea for a bit of target practice? We could make it the best of twenty shots. Mind you, Lenny,' Barney added, stopping to think for a moment, 'you'll have to be handicapped of course, or Lorna and I won't stand a chance of winning against you.'

'We can't tonight,' Lenny answered, with a shake his head. 'Mum's arranged for us all to go to Aunty Edna's house over at Chatmold Park, but we could practise tomorrow afternoon if you like?'

'Yeah, okay then,' said Barney, 'but don't forget to bring some empty cans.'

Suddenly, they heard the cracking sound of gunshots coming from Badger Wood, followed by several cries of rooks and crows as they flew high into the air, cawing loudly.

'Well, I think that we can guess what old Jed's up to now,' muttered Lenny. 'And as usual it's no good! I reckon he's poaching again.'

'Huh! More like, murdering a few dumb animals for a bit of fun,' Lorna replied scornfully.

They continued chatting for a little while and turned to see Jed Hopwood as he suddenly stepped out of the undergrowth.

Dressed in his uncle George's old army jacket and trousers, he was carrying a newly cut branch across his shoulder upon which three dead rabbits were tied, and what appeared to be two small stoats. The children also saw the heads of four cock pheasants sticking out of the large shoulder bag which bounced on Jed's hip.

Cradling his broken-down shotgun across one arm, he approached the three children, giving them all a filthy look from behind his pair of round wire spectacles, which had lenses that reminded Barney of the bottoms of glass lemonade bottles.

Jed Hopwood was twenty years old and was well known in the area for his cruel, loutish behaviour. He was foul mouthed and could hardly utter a complete sentence without cursing something or someone!

Although Jed had a nasty reputation for bullying younger people, like all bullies he chose his targets carefully, but on more than one occasion had come unstuck, against some of his victims' older brother, father or uncle.

His uncle George of course, after the death of Jed's parents, had taken his nephew under his wing and tried desperately to bring the lad up to be kind and decent but wasn't having much success as Jed still remained a lazy no good lout.

Jed, on the other hand, sincerely hoped that his uncle George would soon 'pop his clogs' – as he so quaintly put it! – so that he could inherit his uncle's properties, which would then leave him free to kick out the tenants and sell off their houses and land to greedy property developers. Jed could then have a good time and enjoy wasting his uncle's money. It was therefore quite fair to say that Jed Hopwood was a thoroughly bad lot and not a nice person to be around.

As Jed approached the three children, his face broke into an evil sneer and he growled in a venomous voice, 'What're you nosey little brats staring at? Want some fist do yeh? If there's one thing I can't abide, its nosey little brats like you lot! Go on, buzz off! Or I'll bounce me knuckles off yer 'eads.'

Before he could utter another word, they heard a low growl of warning as Bouncer stepped up menacingly between the three children and the threatening figure of Jed Hopwood.

'Better back off *now*, Hopwood,' shouted Lenny angrily, his blue eyes blazing. 'Bouncer doesn't take too kindly to bully boys.'

'No! Especially if all they can do is pick on kids *half* their age,' Lorna added defiantly.

'Well, well, well,' sneered Jed. 'You little brats really fink you're tough wiv that overgrown teddy bear protecting yeh don't yeh, eh? Well ow'd it be if I put a dirty great 'ole in 'im? Won't be so cocky then will ya?'

'You'll need to load up your gun up first, Jed,' Barney replied, calmly. 'But somehow I don't think that Bouncer's going to give you time.'

'Yeah,' Lenny added. 'I'd be on my way if I were you, before my dad gets to hear about it. I don't think that he'll be as understanding as we are.'

'Why yer cheeky little blighters!' Jed blurted out, and moved towards Lenny threateningly. But before he could take another step, Bouncer leapt up, and with both of his enormous front paws, knocked Jed flat onto his back.

As Jed lay on the ground, his face now totally drained of what little colour he had, Bouncer moved in and straddled the bully's prostrate figure. Slowly moving his head close to Jed's terrified face, Bouncer drew back his lips into a terrifying snarl and let out a loud growl of warning!

Barney and Lorna carefully picked up the shotgun

and game bag, together with the other dead, blood-soaked creatures that had fallen from Jed's grasp, and returned to his cowardly figure lying on the ground. Bouncer still held him in check with a menacing snarl and Jed began to shake with fear!

Lorna gently grasped the shaggy, grey mane on Bouncer's neck and said quietly and calmly, 'You can let him up now, Bouncer, we're quite safe.' The large dog backed off slowly and carefully, still keeping himself between Jed and the three children.

Jed got up off the ground gingerly, and shaking with a mixture of fear and rage, he snarled at them all through gritted teeth, 'I'm gonna make sure that flea-bitten fur ball's put down, you see if I don't. He shouldn't be allowed out! Dangerous, *that's* what he is, lousy, mangy wolf, he ought ter be shot!' Bouncer stepped forward once more and growled menacingly in reply.

'Well, I tell you what, Hopwood,' replied Lenny, pointedly. 'I'm going to let my dad have this gun, and these poor creatures that you've *illegally* killed. When I tell him that you actually threatened us, you know – kids, eleven years of age, *and* threatened to shoot our dog, I'm pretty sure that he'll go to the police.'

'Not to mention the fact that poaching is still a crime in this country, Hopwood. And I bet you don't even have a licence for carrying this gun,' Lorna added, angrily.

'If I were you I'd just buzz off,' Barney suggested, 'before you add any *more* crimes to your list.'

'You lot think you're all so clever, don't yeh, eh? Well you might have won this round but there'll be another time, and we'll *see* then, eh, clever little know it alls.'

Feeling angry and humiliated, Jed Hopwood swore at Barney and the twins and then, glaring murderously at Bouncer, he stormed off down Cat and Kittens Lane, back towards Plummington Minor.

As he disappeared into the distance, the small figure with the keen, jet black eyes, watched him go and suddenly let out a little whoop of delight before disappearing quickly back into the depths of Badger Wood.

Mr Barker was absolutely furious when Barney and the twins informed him about what had occurred that afternoon, and said that he would be 'taking the matter up' with Jed's uncle George. Mr Barker told his wife Rose and the twins that he really didn't want to involve the police if he could avoid it, purely out of the respect that he had for George Hopwood, and the fact that George had tried his best to bring Jed up properly. But he would personally see to it that the gun was destroyed, and that he would be having a quiet word with Jed.

Saturday morning finally came, bright and full of sunshine. Barney dashed down the stairs to find his mum busy cooking breakfast for the two of them on the black leaded range, which served as both a means of cooking and heating the house. Barney absolutely hated it when it had to be cleaned and buffed up with black leaded polish, which was usually *his* job! Olivia was most particular when it came to cleanliness in her house and would say, 'We may not have very much, Barney, but being clean costs nothing but a bit of elbow grease and a little time.'

Barney bolted down his breakfast and as soon he had washed and combed his hair, Olivia and Barney took a leisurely stroll up to Plummington Major. They chose not to take the rickety old bus which was driven by old Mr Pilkington, as his driving tended to make Olivia suffer from travel sickness.

As they made their way along Cat and Kittens Lane they passed various people they knew and exchanged polite greetings: 'Good morning,' or, 'How are you?'

It was a fine summer morning, and ideal for a relaxed walk mixed with a spot of shopping. As they drew near to Badger Wood they could hear the woodland animals chattering and scurrying about noisily.

'Would you just hark at that lot,' Olivia exclaimed. 'Do you know, Barney, there's always been something creepy about that wood. I never liked going in there, even when I was a child. That place has always given me the creeps.'

'Who does the wood belong to, Mum?' asked Barney, looking nervously into the darkness of the trees.

'Well, no one really knows, dear,' she replied with a frown. 'Some people say that it's always belonged to the royal family, but I don't think anyone knows for sure. Now, Barney, I want you to promise me something, son,' she said with deep concern in her voice, 'don't ever go in there on your own, will you?'

'Okay, Mum,' he replied, as he crossed his fingers. 'I won't.' But as he stood there he found that he couldn't tear his eyes away from the dark depths of the wood, and suddenly he had the strangest feeling that something or someone in the wood was calling out to him.

Barney shook off the feeling as he and his mum carried on walking along Cat and Kittens Lane, both of them enjoying the warmth of the sunshine and the scent of the various wild flowers and plants within the hedgerows. Before long they had arrived within the old market town of Plummington Major.

The old town had been around as long as the Doomsday Book, as the locals very often boasted. It was known as one of the oldest market towns in southern England. It certainly had character, although its inhabitants were a strange mix of folk. They were quite friendly and always had a strange tale or two to tell, particularly over a pint of the finest ale at the White Fox Inn, Plummington Major's most popular ale house. The town itself served the local folk who lived in and around Plummington Major and Plummington Minor.

No one could really explain why the two Plummingtons became separate. It was rumoured that there had been a battle between the Minors and the Majors, way back in Plummington's murky past, but no one could honestly say if the tale was true or not. But it did add something to the character of the area, and was always a good tale to tell especially when entertaining visitors or tourists, which very often ended up with the storyteller receiving copious amounts of free ale.
Plummington Major had one main street with a number of little side streets and alleyways that all interconnected forming a maze, which was very easy to get lost in if you didn't know the area.

The town hosted an array of shops and small businesses. Theakstones Bank, the town hall and the Royal Hotel were the largest buildings in the town, while the three inns, the White Fox, the Blue Pig, and the Roebuck, served some of the finest ales that could be found in southern England. There were only two local schools in the area, Plummington Major Junior

School and Plummington Major Senior School.

As Barney and his mum walked along the High Street, they did a little window shopping, stopping occasionally to look closely at some item or other, many of which they simply couldn't afford. But window shopping was a nice way to pass the time and also good therapy for Olivia, even if she didn't always have the money to buy any of the items she had seen.

They found themselves standing outside a rather drab shop with a large bow window, above which hung a dull sign. Its once elegant letters were painted in faded gold leaf, which read 'Crumpshaw's Emporium, purveyor of quality goods and unusual items'.

The shop was old and didn't stand out in any way. In fact it would have been quite easy for people to walk past without noticing that it was there at all!

There were a number of used goods on display outside the shop, which included old prams, tables, vases, old pictures, books, old maps and other assorted bric-a-brac.

Barney and his mum had been browsing the goods that were on offer outside of the shop for a short time, when Barney noticed a rather strange looking cat sitting inside the sunlit window. The cat, who sat next to a set of large, fiery-coloured marbles that Barney had been eyeing up, had quite an elegant air about it as it sat, staring intently into Barney's eyes.

Barney suddenly noticed that the cat only had one eye, which stared back at him from the cat's small face. The odd looking cat was black and white, had dainty little paws, and a fairly large pot belly which hung over its rear paws, almost hiding them from sight as it continued to stare curiously at Barney and his mum.

As Barney pointed out the strange little cat to his

mother, it began to yawn in an almost bored fashion and proceeded to wash and preen itself. Barney asked his mum, 'I wonder what happened to its eye?'

Olivia, who was busy peering into the dark and dusty interior of the shop, replied absently, 'I've no idea. Come on. Let's go inside.'

They made their way into the shop, entering through an old oak door. A shiny brass bell rang out loudly with a deep tinkle, as they both entered, looking for signs of the shop's proprietor.

They stood in the shop for a few moments, gazing at the various items that were for sale and letting their eyes become accustomed to the dimly lit interior. Suddenly the odd little cat jumped down from the window and made its way over to Barney, rubbing its body against his legs. The cat was very friendly and began purring happily, with its tail pointing straight up into the air, as Olivia smiled and said, 'Oh look, Barney; he likes you, isn't that lovely?'

'Oh – it's not a *he*, it's a *she*. In fact,' came a rather quiet but friendly voice from somewhere in the corner of the shop, 'may I introduce you to Tubbsie or should I say Mrs Tubbs, to be more precise.'

They turned around to see a tall, thin figure ambling towards them, and smiled nervously as they saw a rather eccentric looking old man. He had long white hair, a pair of large, bushy eyebrows and a bulbous red nose, upon which a pair of round wire spectacles was perched.

He looked quite odd, odder even than his strange cat. The old man was wearing a bright purple silk smoking cap with a matching jacket, a neat pair of black velvet trousers, and a rather weird looking pair of bright yellow sandals.

They also noticed that he had the most piercing grey eyes that they had ever seen, and gave them both the impression that the old man knew exactly what they were thinking.

'Welcome to my emporium. Please do come in,' said the old man in a soft voice. 'I am the proprietor of this little enterprise,' he added, with a gracious wave of his hands. 'My name is Ezekiel Crumpshaw.' Then he added absently, 'Now, Mrs Tubbs – yes – Mrs Tubbs is my constant companion, and even if I say so myself, is the wisest cat in the world, she always gives me good advice, don't you, Tubbsie?' he continued with a chuckle. 'I really don't know what I would do without her.' Then patting Olivia's arm gently, he said with a smile, 'And how may I be of help to you, madam?'

'Well, it's rather a long story I'm afraid,' she replied. 'But I won't bore you with the details,' she added, feeling a little embarrassed.

'Oh please, madam, do take your time,' said the old man kindly.

'Well,' she said finally, 'It's my son Barney.'

'Ah,' said the man with a smile. 'Broken his bed has he?'

Olivia let out a gasp of amazement. 'But how on earth could you know that?'

'Oh, one gets to find out most things that go on around this neck of the woods.' He smiled meekly. 'It's what keeps me from losing my marbles, you see. You know how it is.' Leaning forward, the old man added with a whisper, 'You are on the lookout for a bed because this young fellow has broken his, am I not correct?'

'Yes we are!' Olivia stammered, quite taken aback, wondering how the old man could possibly have guessed that Barney had broken his bed!

'In that case, I do believe that I may have the very thing that you are looking for,' replied the old man, pointing towards a large, old fashioned oak bedstead.

The old man couldn't fail to notice the crestfallen look on Barney's face, and with a knowing smile said to him, 'It doesn't look like much, does it, young man? But you will find that this bed will be the most comfortable bed you have ever slept on, and it is very strong – oh yes! Even when you use it as a trampoline!' he added, with a sly grin.

Barney felt quite embarrassed and could feel himself blushing. How does he know all this? Barney wondered. This is all very strange.

'Shall we say fifteen shillings and sixpence then, my dear?' The old man asked with an enquiring smile. 'And I'll throw in the mattress and the rather special patchwork quilt of course.'

Before Olivia could utter another word, he said, 'Done! I'll have it delivered to your house later today. Is two thirty okay? Good, we'll call that a deal then, shall we?'

Now befuddled and in a total daze, Olivia handed over the fifteen shillings and sixpence, feeling grateful at how little the oak bedstead had cost her.

She was of course still reeling about how the old man knew all about what had happened regarding Barney's broken bed and began to wonder what *else* he knew!

As they were being led out of the shop by the old man, he leaned over towards Barney and whispered closely into his ear, 'Look after that bed, Barney. I think you will find that it is rather special!' Then turning to Olivia, he said with a formal bow, 'Good day to you, my dear, many thanks for your business, and *please*, do come again.'

He then disappeared back into the dingy shop where he promptly locked the door and put up a large sign the window which read: Gone to Lunch.

As they walked down the High Street, now totally dazed and bemused by the manner of their recent purchase, neither Barney nor Olivia noticed Mrs Tubbs watching them intently through the large bow window of Crumpshaw's Emporium. But then again, no one saw Mrs Tubbs as she suddenly disappeared with twinkle of her one remaining eye!

The journey back to Plummington Minor was uneventful. Both Barney and his mum enjoyed the warmth of the summer sunshine upon their backs once more as they strolled along arm in arm, back down the lane towards home.

'That old Mr Crumpshaw's quite strange, don't you think, Barney?' Olivia asked, with a puzzled frown.

'Yeah he is, Mum,' replied Barney thoughtfully. 'And so is that one-eyed little cat of his, Mrs Tubbs,' he added as he pondered on their visit to Crumpshaw's Emporium.

Barney looked up at his mum and asked, 'Mum, did you get the feeling that old Mr Crumpshaw knew what we were thinking? I mean, how did he know that I needed a new bed?'

'I haven't a clue, son. I honestly don't know,' Olivia murmured in reply. 'The trouble is, Barney, that Plummington's a right place for gossip and news travels fast around here, no matter how trivial it is, and I ought to know, believe me. But never mind that now, we'd better get home and prepare your room for your new bed. I still can't believe how cheap it was,' she added in disbelief. 'All that for fifteen and sixpence, and delivered right to our door. We were really lucky to get such a bargain today, Barney,' she said, sounding very grateful. 'Maybe our luck's changing for the better, eh son?'

'Oh, I really hope so, Mum,' Barney replied meaningfully and gave Olivia's arm a gentle squeeze.

As they approached Badger Wood they could still hear faint cries and calls from deep within the trees.

'Still at it, I hear,' said Olivia. 'I'll bet anything that it's because of that no good Jed Hopwood and what he was up to yesterday.' She looked at Barney and said with a note of warning in her voice, 'Don't you go near him again! He's a bad lot! I'd give him a piece of my mind myself if he wasn't George's nephew, always leering after the women round here, the ugly little brute. It's a good job that Basil sorted him out.'

Barney said nothing as he peered into the darkness of the wood to see if he could spot anything. Olivia looped her arm through his once more and they carried on with their leisurely stroll down the leafy lane towards their tiny cottage.

The small figure of Flitter Trott watched the woman and boy for some time as they disappeared down the lane. Then nimbly jumping down from the branch of the old oak tree he had been hiding in, gave a smile of satisfaction and melted into the darkness of Badger Wood.

Ezekiel Crumpshaw was as good as his word, and at two thirty on the dot, there came a loud rat-a-tat-tat on Olivia's front door. Barney raced down the hallway to answer it, only to find Fred Pritchard, the local milkman, standing on the front doorstep.

Fred was a rather short, stocky man who had been delivering milk to both Plummington Major and Minor for a number of years.

He had short, close-cropped red hair, and a jovial, freckly face. Fred was an ex-Royal Marine, who had the reputation of being quite a tough man and was as strong as an ox.

'Afternoon, young Barney,' said Fred with a jovial smile. 'Is your mum about?'

Olivia appeared at Barney's shoulder and replied cheerfully, 'Oh it's you, Fred – come for your milk money have you?'

'Aye if you've got it to hand, Olivia,' said Fred. 'That'll be grand, but I've got young Barney's bed on the back of me cart and Old Zeke Crumpshaw seemed to know that I was heading this way and asked me to deliver it for him.'

Olivia gave Fred a puzzled look and said, 'Do you know, Fred, it's only just come to me that I never gave Mr Crumpshaw my address, so how did he know where to deliver it?'

Fred scratched his head and replied, 'I dunno, Olivia, that's the way with Old Zeke sometimes. He just sort of knows things; he's always been a bit strange. But he knew I was delivering his milk and decided to ask me. "Can you deliver this to Mrs Betts in Plummington Minor" he said, and here I am!'

Fred gazed down at Barney and said jovially, 'Well! Come on young 'un, let's not let the grass grow under our feet, are you going to give me a hand or not?'

Barney nodded eagerly and helped Fred to unload the large, heavy bedstead, which Fred kindly offered to help Olivia and Barney assemble. It took the three of them the best part of half an hour to put the bedstead together, and it now stood polished and impressive in Barney's bedroom.

'Well I have to say it. That looks a bit-o-quality does that, young 'un,' said Fred, suitably impressed. 'I don't think I've never seen the like of it before. It must be a real antikew.' He meant that the bed was a real antique. Fred had never really been one for using fancy words or reading books!

'Now you remember to take care of it, won't you young 'un?' said Fred earnestly.

'He better had!' Olivia announced, staring at Barney stonily. 'Or there'll be hell to pay! Do you fancy a bacon and egg sandwich while you're here, Fred? Only I'm just going to rustle one up for Barney and me,' Olivia enquired with a smile. 'It'll only take a couple of minutes.'

'Aye, I will, Olivia, if it's not too much trouble, that's very kind of you,' said Fred appreciatively.

When Olivia had disappeared to make the sandwiches, Fred turned to Barney and said, 'I heard from Basil Barker that you and the twins had a bit of bother with that Jed Hopwood yesterday, is that right?'

Before Barney could answer, he saw Fred's nostrils flare as he added, 'Aye, well you steer well clear of Jed Hopwood! He's a slimy little toad, he is. If you have any more truck with him, you tell me and I'll sort him, he's nowt but a bully. He's always been the same, even when he was at school, picking on my little brother an' all.'

'Thanks, Fred,' Barney replied with an awestruck expression, 'but Bouncer's more than a match for him.'

'Aye,' muttered Fred with a grim look on his freckly face, 'that may be, but you be careful of him, he's full-o-spite and wickedness is that one, you just watch out for him that's all.'

Barney's bedroom door opened and Olivia came in with a plate of bacon and egg sandwiches, which had the appearance of large white door steps.

Fred gave Barney a sly wink and said, 'Come on, Barney. It's best that you tuck in before I scoff the lot.' Both Fred and Barney were soon devouring the delicious looking sandwiches ravenously.

'Well, thanks for the nosh, Olivia,' said Fred, after they had eaten. 'Them sandwiches were just what the doctor ordered. Right, I'd better be off now.'

'Thank you very much, Fred,' Olivia replied, 'you really have been ever so kind.'

Then with a grin and a cheery wave Fred stepped outside and climbed aboard his milk cart, then headed back along Cat and Kittens Lane and back towards Plummington Major. Barney was grinning too – at the bit of egg yolk that had been running down Fred's bristly chin!

Barney went back inside and dashed up to his bedroom, where his mum was sorting out some clean sheets to put onto his new bed. She looked at the bright patchwork quilt that had come with the bed and said to Barney, 'I don't know whether to put this quilt on the bed, son. It's a bit old fashioned, don't you think?'

'Oh no, Mum, leave it on, *please* – I really like it and I bet that it'll be ever so warm,' replied Barney eagerly.

'Alright then, Barney,' his mum agreed with a smile. 'Now off you go and play with your pals, your tea is at five thirty, and it's bangers and mash, so *don't* be late.'

Barney ran along the lane to Rosehip Cottage to discover that the twins were helping their father with some weeding in his neatly laid out vegetable garden. Ever since the introduction of food rationing during the war, the Barkers had grown their own fruit and vegetables. The twins' mum was a very thrifty housewife, and had always insisted that her children also learned the finer arts of gardening and cooking.

Mr Barker was a very tall, powerfully built man with large strong hands and enormous feet. He was known locally as the gentle giant, as his gentleness belied his size, and due to the fact that it took a lot for him to lose his temper. However, once he was in a rage, he suddenly became a frightening sight to behold.

'Hello there, young Barney,' said Mr Barker giving him a friendly smile as Barney stepped through the small garden gate. 'How are things with you and your mum? Good I hope?'

'Smashing thanks, Mr Barker,' said Barney, politely. 'Are Lorna and Lenny around?'

'Okay you two off you go and play,' shouted Mr Barker to the twins, who had just appeared from out of the potting shed. 'I'll finish up here,' he added cheerfully, 'but don't be late back for tea or your mother won't be too happy. And remember what I've told you both; keep out of that Jed Hopwood's way; although I don't think he'll try anything like that again, not now that I've had a few choice words with him.'

In the background, unnoticed by any of them, dark black clouds had started to gather, as though a great storm was brewing. The odd thing was that they were only gathering around Badger Wood. Elsewhere the sky was clear and the sun was shining brightly!

~ CHAPTER THREE ~

Dreams, New Friends and Discoveries

Old Zeke Crumpshaw was sitting comfortably in his high backed chair gently stroking the ears of Mrs Tubbs. His face was creased into a worried frown, as he pondered on the news that he had received a few days earlier concerning recent happenings within Badger Wood. The message he had received from the Maiden was quite specific. The Foundling had been taken!

By whom and to where still remained a mystery, and as much as he disliked the idea, it was his responsibility, as one of the Damsel's three guardians, to find the answer to the riddle. Otherwise the consequences for Badger Wood and its creatures, would be catastrophic. It would only then be a matter of time before the Black Wilt would set in, infecting the trees within the haven of Badger Wood. Once that occurred, the pestilence would begin to spread towards outlying areas, incurable and deadly, destroying all vegetation and wildlife in its path.

He looked deeply into the solitary jewel-like eye within Mrs Tubbs' small face, his mind still wrestling with the problem. The answer came to him in an instant; as yet again, the Myrtle Cat had used her telepathic powers to convey a solution upon the old man's worried mind.

'Ah, Tubbsie, as usual you see things very clearly,' he whispered to himself with a chuckle. 'Too clearly for a worn out old man like me. It is all very simple really,' he mumbled to himself as Mrs Tubbs sat licking and preening herself. 'I know that I will have to seek the help of the sprite and the boy, Barnaby Betts, but *who else* can aid us, I wonder?'

At that moment, Old Zeke was aroused from his musings by a sharp rapping upon the shop door. He shuffled slowly to the large bow window and looked out to see his great niece, Katie Crabtree, staring back at him.

'Come on, Uncle! It's only me, open up, please,' begged Katie, peering at Old Zeke through the wavy glass of the window.

'Ah,' the old man chuckled to himself quietly as he unlocked the stout oak door. 'I had forgotten about the school holidays, how fortunate.'

As Katie entered the dimly lit shop, she gave her uncle a huge hug and said, 'Oh it's so good to see you, Uncle. It seems like ages since I last visited you.' With an excited twirl she shouted, 'And now I'm here for *six* whole weeks, isn't that just super?'

'It certainly is, my dear child,' replied Old Zeke, sounding happier than he had been for days. 'Now, I'll just pop the kettle on for a cup of tea and we can have a nice long chat.' Turning around, he disappeared into the parlour with Katie and Mrs Tubbs in tow.

Katie attended Old Fromeston Boarding School for Girls and during her school holidays she came to stay with her great-uncle Ezekiel, because her father worked overseas most of the time and didn't like the idea of dragging Katie all around Europe. Bedsides, the girl needed a good education, which her father felt was only to be found at a good private school.

Although her great-uncle was regarded as rather strange and eccentric by her other relatives, Katie found him very interesting to be around and he seemed to know lots about everything.

Katie's mother, Pandora, had died when she was only five years old, but she too had been very close to Old Zeke, and as he was an uncle on her mother's side of the family, it seemed quite natural for Katie to also be close to the eccentric old man.

Katie was now twelve and although a tall girl she had become quite waif-like during the last year, as she had inherited her mother's slender figure, long, raven hair and dreamy expression.

Ten minutes later Old Zeke and Katie were sitting in the parlour, enjoying a fresh pot of tea, cucumber sandwiches and several slices of whisky fruitcake, which just happened to be one of Katie's favourites.

Katie was sitting comfortably, stroking Mrs Tubbs as she lay curled up on her lap gently purring and snoring. In between munching the fruitcake, Katie told her uncle about the activities she was involved in at school. Old Zeke, as usual, listened patiently, occasionally making a comment or asking her the odd question or two.

During a lull in the conversation Old Zeke leaned forward, and with a seemingly worried expression, asked quietly, 'Katie, I would like you to do something for me, if you will.'

Katie nodded her head slowly, and with a puzzled look on her face replied, 'Why of course I will, Uncle. Is it important?'

'Well,' he answered, 'yes it is,' and very slowly he began to tell Katie of his concerns about Badger Wood and the missing Foundling, and exactly what he needed her to do.

'That was a brilliant shot, Lenny. It must have been at least fifty feet away,' Barney exclaimed, with a howl of delight, as the three children looked at the battered old tin can which now lay on the ground.

Barney and the twins often spent time practising their shooting skills with their homemade catapults. Both Barney and Lorna were considered crack-shots at school, but Lenny easily out-stripped anyone else in Plummington, whether they were a grown-up or a child. They had always practised in a quiet corner of the village green at a safe distance from the windows of the village's houses, and well away from the local duck pond.

There were a number of old fencing posts upon which the children would place old tin cans and then proceed to knock them off with their trusty catapults. This, along with other games like kick the can, marbles and conkers, was a favourite pastime for most of the children who lived in the post-war village of Plummington Minor. However, it has to be said that scrumping pears, apples and plums from Wilf Coggins' orchard was a popular pastime for Barney and the twins. But that was not for the faint hearted as Wilf could be an absolute terror to any scrumpers he caught 'nicking his pears'!

'What we *really* need, are lots of round stones,' said Lenny thoughtfully. 'That way we can be more accurate at a greater distance and there will be far less drag on them as they fly.'

Barney nodded and replied, 'What about our old marbles? They're not much good now because they're all a little bit chipped.'

'They might be worth trying, I suppose,' Lorna agreed giving them both a rueful smile, 'but I don't think it'll help us beat old crack-shot Willy here.'

'We'll give it a try tomorrow, then,' Barney replied. 'My marbles have just about had it anyway, and besides, I don't really mind wasting one or two. I saw a really nice set of new ones in that old junk shop in Plummington Major this afternoon, they looked ever so good, and my pocket money's due this week so I may be able to buy some new ones.'

'What! Do you mean old Mr Crumpshaw's shop?' Lorna asked looking a little surprised. Barney nodded and Lorna smiled and said, 'He goes into my dad's bank sometimes. My dad says that he's really nice but little bit odd, *if* you know what I mean.'

'Didn't you get your new bed from there?' asked Lenny.

'Yeah,' replied Barney. 'You should see it though, it's huge, and I bet it'll sleep three people easily. Anyway, we could go up to the shop on Monday if you like and have a look at those marbles.'

'Yeah, why not?' replied Lenny. 'It'll be nice to have a dekko in that shop; there always seems to be a lot interesting stuff in the window, and to be honest, I've always wanted to have a good nose around in there.'

'Me too,' added Lorna earnestly. 'I bet there's all sorts

of strange, weird things in that place. Ooh – I wonder if it's like "The Old Curiosity Shop", you know like the one in that book which we've been reading in school.'

'Okay,' said Barney, 'It's agreed then, we'll go there on Monday; I can't wait! I just hope that I can persuade Mum to give me the money to get those marbles.'

That evening, an excited Barney lay tucked up snugly in his new bedstead and quickly sank into a deep sleep. Before very long he was snoring gently and he began to dream.

Barney dreamt that he was flying high up in the air on his new bedstead and that it was raining very heavily, but strangely, he didn't feel any rain and he certainly wasn't getting wet. After a time he looked down and saw that he was flying over a rugged mountain landscape which appeared to be surrounded by a dense mist and dangerous looking marshland.

Strange, dark, shadowy creatures with wicked green eyes kept flitting in and out of his dream and they appeared to be acting cruelly towards a tiny furry white animal, but he couldn't see it very clearly, as the evil looking creatures seemed to be trying to drive him away.

Barney's dream changed suddenly as he seemed to have stopped flying and the bedstead was now floating in mid-air. He found himself staring down upon the sad figure of an old man, who bore a strange resemblance to old Mr Crumpshaw. He appeared to be sitting alone, cold and wet, with his head bent, deep in thought.

His dream changed once more, as the dark shadowy creatures appeared again and he felt pairs of warty, dark hands clawing at him as though they were trying to drag him down into an evil, smelling dark hole, located deep within the dangerous looking marshland!

Barney awoke suddenly with a start, his body covered with sweat and he lay there for a while, wondering where he was. Slowly as he came fully round from his world of sleep, Barney realised that he was safely at home in bed. 'Gordon Bennett! What a nightmare that was!' he exclaimed in a hoarse whisper.

He continued to lie there for a little while, within the covers of the brightly coloured patchwork quilt, thinking about his strange dream, when he suddenly heard his mother shout, 'Barney, time to get up. Your breakfast's on the table.'

Barney's thoughts came instantly back to food. 'Great! I'm starving,' he mumbled to himself and quickly jumped out of bed. After getting dressed in record time, he dashed down the stairs and into the kitchen to eat.

'My, my, you're in a hurry this morning. Did you sleep well last night, son?' his mum asked cheerfully. 'Only I heard you talking and moaning in your sleep during the night.'

'Fine thanks, Mum,' replied Barney through a mouthful of hot, buttered toast.

'Barney, how many times do I have to tell you? Don't speak with your mouth full,' cried his mum with a shake of her head. 'Now, after you've eaten, get yourself washed and ready for church, and *don't* forget to comb your hair, it looks a mess, and for heaven's sake *don't* dawdle! We're late as it is.'

Barney gazed up at his mum from the table, and replied in his meekest voice, 'Okay, Mum.'

In a flash Barney suddenly remembered his pocket money, and swallowing a large mouthful of toast, said quickly, 'Mum? Can I have my pocket money today, please? Only, I want to buy some new marbles, mine have just about had it.' Before his mum could reply he added, 'Lorna and Lenny are going to buy some new ones as well.'

Olivia gazed at the pleading look in her son's eyes and answered softly, 'Barnaby Betts! I am *not* made of money, you know,' and then with a relenting smile she added, 'Yes, alright then, but you're going to have to earn it! You can begin by helping me in the garden this afternoon,' and then with an exasperated sigh she went off to get herself ready for church.

A little while later the two of them were walking down the lane into Plummington Minor, heading towards the 12th century church of Saint Cuthbert which stood close to the village green. As they approached the old church, they saw the tall but prim figure of Agnes Holfirth, who nodded politely as she greeted them both. 'Good morning, Olivia, and good morning to you, Barnaby.' Then after giving him a rather searching look she asked, 'Is everything alright with you, young man?'

'Yes Miss Holfirth,' replied Barney, sounding a little puzzled. 'I'm fine thanks.'

However, Barney couldn't help noticing the strange looks that Miss Holfirth gave him all the way through the Sunday morning service.

As Barney and his mum made their way out into the churchyard they ran into Mr and Mrs Barker and the twins, and while Olivia chatted to Rose and Basil, Barney and the twins went and sat upon the church boundary wall.

'Fancy a spot of fishing later, Barney?' Lorna asked. 'Kevin Oliver reckons that there are loads of sticklebacks in Dingle Brook.'

'Nah – I can't,' replied Barney, glumly. 'I've got to help Mum in the garden, I have to *earn* my pocket money, she says.'

'Oh that's tough. Well, never mind,' said Lenny. 'At least you'll be able to buy those marbles, won't you? And we can always go fishing another day.'

After an afternoon's hoeing and weeding the vegetables in Olivia's cottage garden, Barney was feeling totally worn out, but happy as his mother had given him his pocket money and a little extra. Later that evening he tumbled exhausted into bed and very quickly fell fast asleep.

He had the same dream again, about the strange land and the old man, and woke up just before the dark shadowy creatures could pull him down from his bedstead. 'Blimey. That was really scary,' he mumbled to himself, as he got dressed and prepared to go to Plummington Major with the twins.

A little while later, as the three children were walking along Cat and Kittens Lane, Barney told them about his strange dreams.

'Maybe you're turning into a raving loony,' Lenny mused thoughtfully as he gave Barney a grin.

'And maybe he'll be in good company, Lenny – especially with you around,' replied Lorna mischievously. 'Mind you – I *do* think that it all sounds a bit odd.'

'Yeah and so is that,' announced Lenny, staring up at the dark storm clouds, which now hung like a dark black cloak over Badger Wood. 'It's been like that for nearly two days now.' The three children gazed curiously into the sky and moved quickly along the lane towards Plummington Major.

'Here they are!' cried Barney as the three children peered into the window of Crumpshaw's Emporium. There, in a brown canvas bag, which lay partly open, sat a shiny set of fiery looking marbles.

'Ooh, they do look pretty,' yelled Lorna excitedly. 'Come on, let's go inside and see how much they are.'

As they stepped inside the dimly lit shop, the brass doorbell gave its customary deep tinkle and the children heard the sound of a dreamy voice coming from the corner of the shop's interior, 'Oh, hello – can I help you?'

As they looked around to find out who the owner of the voice was, they saw a tall, slender looking girl, who appeared to be roughly the same age as they were, standing staring at them and giving them all a pleasant smile.

'Umm, well, we were wondering about those marbles in the window,' Barney stammered as he pointed to the bag of fiery glass spheres.

At that moment old Mr Crumpshaw, came in from the rear of the shop, followed closely by Mrs Tubbs, who walked up to Barney and rubbed her body up against his legs.

'Ah! It's young Barney if I am not mistaken,' said Old Zeke. 'And how is your dear mother?' Then giving him a nod and a sly wink the old man asked, 'But more importantly, how is your bed? You are sleeping well, I trust?'

'Er, fine thank you, Mr Crumpshaw,' replied Barney politely.

'Now then, who are these wonderful children?' asked Old Zeke. 'Friends of yours, Barney?'

'Yes,' replied Barney and proceeded to introduce Lorna and Lenny.

'Good, good,' replied the old man, his piercing grey eyes twinkling merrily. 'Do you know, it's so very nice, to see such happy young folk in my emporium. You all brighten up the old place.'

They all stared at one another sheepishly as Old Zeke continued, 'This is my niece, Katie Crabtree,' he said, introducing the tall girl, with a wave of his hand. 'I would certainly deem it a great favour, Barney, if you and your chums would consider becoming friends with Katie. She doesn't know any of the other children from around here, and it really would make her holidays so much more interesting, don't you think?'

Lorna, Lenny and Barney looked surprised, but nodded their heads in agreement.

'Good! Then I will leave you in her very capable hands,' he added with a smile of satisfaction, and with a wave of his hand disappeared into the back of the shop.

'The marbles are nine pence a bag, if that's okay?' said Katie, as she placed several bags upon the counter.

'Oh! Yeah, brilliant,' replied Lenny with a grin. 'I thought that they'd cost us a lot more than that, so we'll all have two bags each please, Katie,' he said as he looked at Lorna and Barney who nodded in agreement.

After the money had been handed over, the four children chatted for a while about their schools and what interests they all had in common. They slipped into conversation very easily with Katie, and discovered that she had an uncanny knack of putting them all at ease. Lorna and Katie took an immediate liking to each other, so much so that Lorna suddenly exclaimed, 'It's going to be nice not to be outnumbered by boys, for once.'

'But you're *almost* a boy anyway, Lorna,' replied Lenny with a laugh, moving quickly out of punching range.

The sound of the children's merry laughter floated into the High Street as Mrs Tubbs moved around each of the children, purring in delight at the sound of their merriment.

Katie picked her up and Mrs Tubbs snuggled tightly into her neck, purring noisily. Katie said dreamily, 'She's a very special cat you know, and also very magical!'

Barney and Lenny exchanged amused glances as Lenny, who was now smirking slyly, felt a sharp nudge in his ribs from Lorna's elbow.

'Oh, you probably think that I'm *quite* mad,' Katie said, with a wry smile, 'but it's true, Tubbsie is in fact a Myrtle Cat, and comes from a faraway magical world.'

Lenny felt as if he was almost fit to burst as he thought to himself, is she mad? Barney simply stood there stunned, not knowing quite what to think.

Lorna smiled and replied, 'Well *I* believe you, Katie,' as she stared stonily at Barney and Lenny. 'I tell you what, how would you like to meet up with us tomorrow, maybe we could do a bit of exploring together? It would be great fun. We could meet you at the top of Cat and Kittens Lane, that's if you're up for it?'

'Okay,' Katie replied. 'I would like that *very* much. Tomorrow morning it is then! Maybe I can tell you a bit more about my uncle and Mrs Tubbs.'

On their way back home Lenny said, 'That Katie's a bit of an odd one, don't you think? I mean, Myrtle Cat! I *ask* you.'

'Oh, stop being so rude, Lenny,' Lorna replied testily. 'I happen to think that she's very nice, a little strange, yes, but very nice.

'What do you think, Barney?' Lorna asked, with a sly smile as she gave him a sideways glance.

'Er – I think she's very nice too,' Barney replied, avoiding the look of shock on Lenny's face.

'Well,' said Lenny with a resigned shrug of his shoulders and a shake of his head. 'Are we going to try shooting our old marbles this afternoon or what?'

Barney just mumbled, 'Yeah,' as he kept his eyes down, his mind still pondering about the strange but likable Katie Crabtree.

That afternoon Barney and the twins spent time either throwing sticks for Bouncer or shooting at the tin cans perched on top of the fence posts on the village green. They soon found that by using their old marbles as ammunition, they could hit the tin cans with almost every shot and from much further away. They did lose one or two old marbles mind you, but were more than happy with their new discovery.

As Lorna was throwing sticks for Bouncer to chase, they suddenly heard a loud squawking from behind a large clump of gorse bushes at the edge of the village green.

They heard the loud cursing voice of Jed Hopwood shouting, 'Keep still blast yer! Ya noisy little blighter.'

The children crept up to take a closer look and saw Jed's backside sticking out from a thick clump of bushes as he gripped the neck of a large wild duck tightly with both his hands, plainly trying to strangle it!

'Let's set Bouncer on him,' cried Lorna angrily.

'No, leave him to us,' replied Barney with a whisper, and very carefully, he and Lenny loaded their catapults with two of the old marbles. Slowly, they both pulled back the elastic to their chins and aiming very carefully, they released their elastics simultaneously and let the marbles fly.

Almost instantly Jed bellowed loudly in pain, as he quickly released the wild duck.

The unfortunate creature, having escaped from its murderous captor, instantly took flight with a loud squawk. Flapping its wings until it was high above the bushes, the duck then flew off into the fields beyond the village green.

Barney and the twins fell about holding their sides with silent laughter when they saw Jed emerge from the bushes, holding both cheeks of his backside, as he limped away painfully with an angry look on his face.

'Oh, they were the best shots ever!' shouted Lorna, looking really impressed. 'Did you see his face?' The tears of mirth were now rolling down Lenny's cheeks as he lay on the grass thumping the ground. He raised his head and wheezed breathlessly, 'Look, he's still limping.'

'It jolly well serves him right,' Lorna cried. 'The great brute! How could he do that to a poor defenceless animal?'

'That's because he's a big stupid idiot,' replied Barney wiping the tears of laughter from his eyes. 'But maybe he'll think twice before he does it again!'

Later that evening, after his bedtime mug of hot cocoa, Barney climbed the stairs to bed wondering whether he would have the same dream again. He snuggled down under the quilted bedclothes, smiling to himself about everything that had happened that day. Sleepily, he whispered to himself, 'Ah, to bed and away.'

Almost instantly he sat up, now wide awake again,

certain that he had felt his bedstead move. His eyes grew wide in horror as he saw the wall opposite his bed magically melt away until it had completely disappeared!

Barney rubbed his eyes in disbelief, wondering if he was dreaming again.

Then, very slowly but surely he felt the bedstead lift itself off the floor and move steadily forward out of his bedroom into Cat and Kittens Lane.

Before he knew it, the bed began to climb up into the sky, gradually picking up speed as it flew. Then quite suddenly it changed direction and began to fly in a large circle around Plummington Minor.

As the bedstead spiralled steadily higher and higher, the village appeared to become quite small. Thinking that he was about to fall, Barney tightly gripped the rail at the head of his bedstead.

It now began to rain quite heavily, but Barney noticed that somehow he wasn't getting wet, but then again he couldn't feel any wind either. He saw various people that he knew who lived in the village, walking home from the village inn. Yet no matter how loudly he shouted for them to come and rescue him, no-one seemed to see or hear him!

The bed began to slow down a little to a more comfortable speed and began to carry out a number wide turns as it banked both to the left and to the right. Barney found that after several minutes of the bedstead flying around Plummington, his fears of tumbling back to earth were groundless, as his bed did a huge, but graceful, loop the loop! Somehow his bedstead prevented him from falling and he began to relax a little, moving his body so that he was kneeling in a more stable position.

Barney soon found that if he leaned very carefully

to one side or the other of the bedstead he could make it bank to the right or to the left. If he leaned back a little, the bedstead would slowly begin to climb and when he leaned forwards it would slowly descend towards the ground.

As the time passed, Barney became accustomed to the movements of the bedstead and began to enjoy his ride, and for three hours or more Barney practised steering his bed, until he could control it almost by thought.

After flying around Plummington Minor several more times he decided to try out various manoeuvres once more, and was really thrilled with his new discovery. Eventually he decided to head back home and began to guide the bedstead back towards Cat and Kittens Lane.

He was so excited and muttered to himself, 'Just wait until the twins hear about this!' No sooner had he uttered the words, his bedstead suddenly gave a stomach churning lurch and rapidly began to soar high into the storm clouds far above. Then just as quickly, the bedstead finally stopped and remained motionless in the darkness for several seconds. Suddenly, with another stomach churning lurch, it began travelling like a rollercoaster, as it plunged at breakneck speed towards the heart of Badger Wood.

~ CHAPTER FOUR ~

Flitter Trott

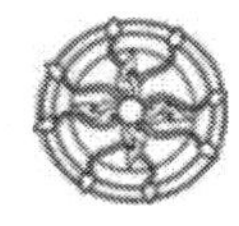

Barney cried out in fear as his bedstead plummeted towards the ground. He was still amazed that he hadn't tumbled out of the bedstead as it continued dropping like a stone. Strangely, Barney had somehow remained in the same comfortable kneeling position on the bedstead, no matter how fast his bed flew, whether it climbed steeply, turned sharply, or dive-bombed towards the ground! He could only assume that it was all a part of the bed's magic.

Down and down, the bedstead continued its relentless dive towards Badger Wood. Barney's eyes widened in terror, as the leafy branches of the trees grew nearer and although it seemed like a long time, it had only taken a few seconds for the bedstead to reach the dark interior of Badger Wood.

Barney saw that he was heading towards a large

grass covered hill within the middle of the wood, but still the bedstead showed no signs of slowing down. As the large hill loomed nearer and nearer, Barney braced himself for an almighty crash. 'Oh crumbs, now I'm for it!' he gulped helplessly.

However, at the moment of impact, instead of the expected bone crunching crash, he was surrounded by a loud whooshing sound.

To his utter astonishment, Barney gasped as the hillside suddenly dissolved in front of him, and the bedstead quickly levelled out as he regained control once more.

Barney looked around him and found that he was now flying in an unfamiliar landscape. 'Oh heck, where am I?' he mumbled to himself in a panic. Feeling very unsure and fearful he shouted out desperately, 'Bed! Please stop!'

The bedstead halted and as if held by invisible wires, floated motionless in mid-air.

'Whew, that was some ride,' he muttered to himself, as he wiped the sweat from his face. Barney breathed a little more easily, as he slowly gazed all about him and saw the range of craggy mountains which spread out before him, as far as his eyes could see.

Leaning forward slightly, Barney brought the bedstead to land gently in a large valley which lay within the middle of the mountain range. As he looked ahead he noted that the mountains gave the appearance of being carved from of gigantic blocks of dark glass, probably caused by some ancient volcanic upheaval.

Barney was about to climb down from the bedstead to stretch his legs and explore a while, when he suddenly heard a voice inside his head, which sounded strangely like Miss Holfirth's, warning him to be careful and to stay on the bedstead. Thinking about it for a moment he decided to remain where he was, as his bed seemed to be the safest place, for the present at least.

It didn't take long for Barney to realise that he had seen these mountains before, and he murmured aloud, 'Hey! I know these mountains; they're the ones I've been dreaming about for the past two nights!'

He cast his eyes around him once more, and in the pale grey twilight observed that there were shadows dotted here and there. Instinctively Barney noticed that some of the shadows appeared to be moving towards him. As he strained his eyes to see the moving shadows more clearly, he suddenly heard a voice hissing loudly, as it echoed in the valley, 'What are you doing here, boy? What is it that you are looking for?'

The voice sounded frightening and sent a chill up Barney's back, and although it seemed to be coming from far away, Barney felt certain that its owner was very close.

Now looking around him frantically, Barney saw that the shadows were moving towards him with an eerie, gliding motion. Their clawed outstretched hands were reaching for him, as he caught a glimpse of their wicked green eyes and pointed fangs, within their dark, warty faces.

The voices hissed harshly, as Barney cried out in a terrified voice, 'Who *are* you?'

'We are who we are, boy,' the voices taunted. 'Come with us and let us take you to the deep dark places of our realm!'

At that precise moment, Barney found his courage once more and roared fiercely, 'Not on your Nelly! I'm off!'

Then as several pairs of hands reached out to drag him down, he shouted loudly, 'Bed! Get me out of here, *now*!'

At once, and as though the bedstead sensed that Barney was in mortal danger, it shot up like a rocket, high into the purple-blue sky and, stopping for a split second, plunged again at lightning speed back towards the ground. The creatures were scattered and flew in all directions, as with a wide sweeping turn, the bedstead headed off into the night!

Barney flew for several minutes before the bedstead climbed high into the sky once more before stopping suddenly in mid-air. It hung in the sky for a second or two and then plummeted into the side of a gigantic snow topped mountain.

Barney closed his eyes tightly and once again heard the loud whooshing sound as he waited for the inevitable crash. But when he opened his eyes, he found himself high in the sky once more, looking down upon Badger Wood.

With a huge sigh of relief, Barney shook his head and shouted, 'Bed! *Please* take me home!'

In no time at all, he found himself back in his bedroom, which, to his great surprise, appeared as it always had done. The wall opposite his bedstead had magically repaired itself and looked as though nothing at all had happened.

Barney's head flopped down onto his large fluffy pillow, and as he lay there shaking his head in disbelief he became very tired. Before he knew it he had fallen asleep and was snoring loudly.

Next morning Barney awoke quite suddenly to the sound of his mother calling from below. 'Barney, time to get up! Come on, lazy bones – your breakfast is on the table.'

He sat up, rubbed the sleep from his eyes and mumbled to himself, 'Crikey that was some dream.' Then sitting blearily on the side of his bed, he started to get dressed, and suddenly noticed that there were broken bits of twigs and leaves stuck between the curved, rails and rungs at the end of his bedstead. Barney scratched his head thoughtfully and then suddenly realised that he hadn't been dreaming at all!

Later that morning, Barney and the Barker twins were waiting at the turning into Cat and Kittens Lane for Katie Crabtree to arrive.

'Are you sure, that you *weren't* dreaming again, Barney?' Lenny asked seriously.

'No! I've *told* you,' Barney replied impatiently. 'I found twigs and leaves stuck in the end of my bed, didn't I? And how on earth could they have got there if it was only a dream?'

Lenny shrugged his shoulders and replied grimly, 'I don't know, mate, honestly I don't.'

Lorna gave Barney, a sideways glance and said, 'Look, Barney, we really *do* believe you, you know that don't you? But it all sounds a bit, well – far-fetched, if you know what I mean?'

At that moment the tall, dark-haired figure of Katie Crabtree came striding towards them, and with a beaming smile she shouted, 'Hello everyone, been waiting long? I must say, it's a fair old walk to get here isn't it?'

'I'm surprised that you didn't get Mrs Tubbs to conjure up a magic carpet for you,' Lenny spluttered, giving Lorna a sly wink.

'What with you *and* Barney, you could both set up your own magical Air Force.'

'Oh, Lenny, don't be so cruel!' Lorna scolded, as she noticed Barney, staring at the ground, as if deep in thought.

'Quite a charmer, isn't he?' said Katie sarcastically, giving Lenny a sickly sweet smile.

'Aw, come on, I was only joking,' Lenny complained. 'I mean, you *can* take a joke, can't you?'

Barney suddenly stared at them all and said seriously, 'Shut up and listen a minute – I want to go into the wood!'

Lorna and Lenny looked at Barney in surprise asked, 'You don't mean Badger Wood, do you, Barney?'

'Yeah, of course I do, where else do you think I want to go?' he replied, with a frown.

'I don't fancy going in there,' muttered Lenny, looking distinctly uneasy. 'It's a weird place, and don't forget the promise you made to your mum.'

Barney cocked his head to one side and grinned. 'I promised Mum that I wouldn't go in there *alone*, remember? But if you're all too scared to come along…'

Hang on a minute!' Lenny retorted. 'Who said anything about being scared?'

'Barney,' Lorna asked seriously, as she pointed towards Badger Wood. 'why on earth do you want go in there?'

'Let's just say that I feel as I ought to,' he teased, his eyes full of excitement. 'Are you coming or not?'

'Ooh! I do love an adventure, don't you?' Katie crooned, as though she was daring the twins to say no.

Lenny nodded giving Barney a smile 'Okay – you're on!'

'Well, it looks like that's *settled* then,' Barney announced triumphantly!

The four children decided to enter Badger Wood through the Crossway, a little dirt track which led down to the bridge that crossed over the Dingle Brook.

'We'll pick up Bouncer on the way,' Lorna suggested, now excited at the prospect of an adventure. 'Oh, you'll just *love* him, Katie – he's absolutely bonkers.'

Lenny turned to Lorna and Barney and asked them if they had their catapults with them. With a grin, Barney and Lorna produced the 'Y' shaped sticks from the back pockets of their cotton shorts. Barney also pulled out his bag of marbles, with a flourish, from one of his other pockets and smiling impishly said, 'We mustn't forget the ammo.'

About half an hour later the four children, now followed by Bouncer, strolled leisurely along the Crossway and across the rickety old bridge. The water within Dingle Brook was murky after the recent heavy rainfall, and babbled merrily as it meandered through the wood before disappearing amongst the trees, far ahead.

As the children continued walking they could almost feel a great pall of sadness emanating from within wood itself, as slowly but surely, they made their way along the tiny path and into the wood's brooding interior.

'Our dad will go mad if he knows that we're in here,' said Lorna nervously.

'So would my mum,' Barney whispered. 'She wouldn't half give me what for!'

'Even Bouncer's quiet,' Lenny noted, as they observed the large grey dog casually sniffing amongst the undergrowth, as unconcerned as ever. 'You know, I reckon that he comes in here every day,' Lenny mused, as he walked with his hands shoved deeply into his pockets.

'Oh, I've been in here before, *loads* of times,' said Katie dreamily. 'When I was little, I often came with my uncle Ezekiel.' She turned to see that the other three children had stopped and stood gaping at her with open mouths. 'Of course Uncle Ezekiel was a bit younger then and he used to come in here all the time.'

'But weren't you ever afraid?' asked Lorna.

'No – not really,' Katie replied. 'I always had Uncle Ezekiel with me, and he has loads of friends within this wood.'

'Friends?' asked Barney, giving Katie a puzzled stare.

'Well, you know, the animals – sprites and things,' replied Katie earnestly.

Lenny and Barney tried hard to smother the smirks of laughter that were beginning to crease the corner of their mouths, as they gave each other a 'here she goes again' look.

As they walked deeper into Badger Wood, Barney and the twins were still thinking about what Katie had told them. Barney was just about to ask her what a sprite was, when they heard the noise of something or someone moving around noisily within the bushes in front of them. Lenny and Barney quickly drew their catapults from their back pockets and in a flash had them loaded and ready to fire, just in case they had run into Jed Hopwood.

Bouncer, on the other hand, was barking away merrily as his tail wagged excitedly from side to side.

Lorna stepped forward and shouted loudly, 'Come on out! Whoever you are! We know that you're in there.'

The bush immediately in front of them began to shake excitedly and gave a loud giggle!

Barney and Lenny aimed their catapults shakily and cried, 'If you don't come out now, we'll shoot!'

The bush began to shake more vigorously and the giggling grew louder still, as Bouncer began to whimper with excitement his tail began to wag even faster.

Suddenly a mischievous voice cried out with mirth, 'Oh, please don't, I'm already doubled up with laughter and the two of you will most probably miss, and I can hardly stand up properly for laughing as it is!'

Then from out of the bush, stepped the strangest creature that the children had ever seen.

A tiny little man now stood before them, he was only half as tall as the children. The man was staring at them all quite intently with a pair of keen, jet black eyes, and appeared to be highly amused at their discomfort.

He was dressed in the most outlandish clothes that the children had ever laid eyes upon; he wore an earth-brown coloured tunic, short, leafy-green trousers, topped off with an absurd little red hat that covered his straw coloured hair. In short, he appeared like something out of a pantomime.

Quite suddenly, he leapt into the air clicking the heels of his tiny brown leather boots together. As he did so, he laughed and pointed at the children. 'Hah! Hah! Hah! Got you there didn't I? What's the matter? Cat got your tongues, has it?'

Barney and the twins stood rooted to the spot, unable to believe what they were seeing and were totally mesmerized by the antics of the little fellow, who was now laughing uncontrollably.

None of them however had noticed that Katie was now leaning against an oak tree with her arms folded, staring at them all with a highly amused expression.

'Well, well. If it isn't young Katie Crabtree! Come up to visit me after *all* these years,' cried the little man with glee. '*And* you've brought some friends along as well, now isn't that just grand.'

Katie stepped forward and turning to Barney and the twins, said, 'My friends, allow me to introduce you to the one and only Flitter Trott! He is one of the guardians of Badger Wood.'

The strange little man smiled at the children and removed his tiny red hat with a flourish. After a deep bow he said, 'I'm pleased to meet you all at last. Flitter Trott, at your service.'

Barney and the twins gazed at Flitter Trott in wonder, not quite believing their eyes. 'Excuse me, sir,' asked Barney politely, 'but, what sort of creature are you?'

Flitter Trott sauntered over to Bouncer, on his stick-like legs, and began to nuzzle his bearded face against Bouncer's nose, before replying, 'Why, I'm a wood sprite, of course, *even* young Bouncer here knows that! Don't you, boy?' He turned and gave them all a mischievous smile. Been watching you three for ages, so I have,' he said, pointing to Barney and the twins. 'And especially, *you* young Barnaby Betts! Oh don't look so shocked,' he added giving them a sly smile.

'How did you know who we were? And how do you know our dog?' demanded Lenny.

Flitter Trott placed both hands on his narrow hips, and with his feet planted apart explained, 'You children don't *listen* do you? As I have told you, I've been watching you all for a *long* time, from the time that you all took your first steps, as a matter of fact!' He caught the look of astonishment reflected in their eyes, and with a chuckle of amusement added teasingly, 'What's the matter? Cat got your tongues again?'

'Flit,' Katie asked quite seriously, 'what's been going on, here in the wood?'

'What indeed,' replied Flitter Trott grimly. 'I expect that Ezekiel has sent you all to help out eh?'

'Well, yes he has, Flit,' Katie answered seriously. 'My uncle had heard that the Foundling has been taken and asked me to offer you what help I could.'

'So why didn't he come himself?' Flitter Trott asked suspiciously.

'Look, Flit,' replied Katie firmly, 'Uncle Ezekiel can't move around like he used to, he's really old now you know, and he's relying more on Mrs Tubbs and the Maiden these days – and bedsides he's got *me* hasn't he?'

'Humph, I suppose he has,' admitted the wood sprite, grudgingly. 'The only help I seem to get these days is from young Bouncer here, and I must say, that is a very clever dog that you have there,' he added, nodding at Lorna and Lenny. 'He comes and keeps watch for me every day, he does, don't you, Bouncer?' Bouncer's tail was wagging happily as he replied with a loud bark.

Lorna stared at Bouncer in amazement, hardly believing what she had seen, or what Flitter Trott had told them about their *own* pet dog.

'Mister Trott,' Lorna asked politely, 'how did you get Bouncer to help you? I mean, he doesn't wander up to just *anyone*, does he, Lenny?' Her twin brother simply shook his head in reply.

Flitter Trott looked at the twins, his eyes now dancing with amusement, and replied, 'Bouncer just happened to come up to me one day and offered me his help. You see, I can tell what animals are thinking and I can also speak to them, in my *own* way of course. That's because I'm a wood sprite see.' He paused for a moment and then continued, 'Oh, and by the way, let's not stand on ceremony – just call me Flit.'

Barney, who had been standing quietly looking at Flitter Trott, Katie and Bouncer in wonder, suddenly asked, 'Flit? What do you know about my magic bedstead?'

'Ah,' Flitter Trott replied knowingly. 'I thought that we might get around to that sooner or later. All that I'll say for the moment is that it was no accident that you came by the bed-scapator.'

'The what?' replied Barney and the twins together.

'Enough!' ordered Flitter Trott suddenly. 'This isn't really the place to be talking about this. Trees have ears you know,' he continued, giving them a nod and a sly wink. Then with a beckoning wave of his hand, he started to run along the path that led deeper into the heart of the wood. 'Follow me,' he called out cheerfully, as he danced along the path in front of them. 'We'll talk about this somewhere safer.'

The four children followed the wood sprite as quickly as they could, while Bouncer padded alongside them, barking merrily. Flitter Trott disappeared along the path and every now and then they could hear his musical voice in the distance taunting them merrily, 'Come along you slowcoaches, not far to go now.'

They carried on half running and walking for a time, still hearing Flitter Trott's occasional shouts, until suddenly they emerged into a small clearing and saw the wood sprite standing before a very large, ancient oak tree.

Breathing heavily, they saw that Flitter Trott had his hands on his hips and was laughing jovially as he taunted them, 'Still with me I see, my young friends. Well, you finally made it at last, eh. Welcome to Goblin Oak! This is where I live, well most of the time anyway.' With a wave of his hand, a small green door appeared within the trunk of the giant tree. It had a large shiny brass knocker, shaped like the leering face of a goblin stuck in the centre of door.

One at a time, the children crawled through the opening. As Barney entered he could have sworn the door knocker's ugly little face bobbed out its tongue, blew him a loud raspberry and then squeaked in a high pitched voice. 'Come along, you little slug! Get a move on!'

Once inside, the children found themselves in a large spacious room. At one end of the room there were a number of large, comfortable looking armchairs and a shiny copper kettle which was perched upon an old black pot stove. It whistled away merrily to the tune of 'Here we go gathering nuts in May'.

They sat down on the brightly coloured armchairs, and very soon were happily drinking hot, sweet tea and munching on delicious slices of caraway seed cake, while Bouncer lay curled up next to the little pot stove enjoying its warmth.

As they all sat there, tucking in to the scrumptious food, Flitter Trott looked at each of the children in turn, his jet black eyes sparkling with energy.

Suddenly he spoke quite loudly, making them all jump. 'Well! I suppose you had better know why you have been brought here and what strange things have been happening in this wood.' He paused to let his words sink in, and to make sure that he had got everyone's full attention, before continuing, 'I *suppose* I had better start at the beginning,' and slowly, Flitter

Trott began to tell them his tale.

Meanwhile, deep within the Rotten Marshes, close to the Stag Mountains, a large group of shadowy creatures with wicked looking green eyes were listening intently to their chieftain Faraak, as he held his brethren's gaze within his own powerful presence.

'Brothers, we have at last, come to the time where we will soon have the magic which will enable us all to take control of Pangloria.' His Bogwight brethren hissed and howled in reply to their leader, some licking their long white fangs, in greedy anticipation of the revenge which was to come.

'Brothers, oh brothers,' Faraak continued, 'The Three Moon Equinox is fast approaching, and as you all know, three full moons occurring at the same instant, happens only once every thousand years. *Yessss*,' he hissed with relish, 'it will soon be time to sacrifice the Foundling and once we have the essence of her magic for ourselves we can take our rightful place in Pangloria and rule unchallenged!'

As he held the Bogwight brethren within his baleful gaze he continued with a hissing rasp, 'Yes, very soon, my brothers, we will have two whole worlds to feed upon.' The large group of Bogwights hissed and howled jubilantly in response.

In the lonely Valley of the Fiery Holes, deep within the Stag Mountains, sat the lonely figure of Rookwort. His slim frame was bent over, as if he had taken a great load upon his aged shoulders. The valley was named after the three large volcanic fissures, which lay like gaping, fiery wounds at its southern end.

The Fiery Holes were prone to minor eruptions and

from time to time, would belch out small amounts of hot lava and sulphurous smoke, and as a result, people and other creatures tended to avoid coming into the valley. This suited the old man's purpose, as he tended to shun the company of others, mainly because he trusted very few people or other sentient beings. Here at least, he would be left alone.

Rookwort sat deep in thought, still admonishing himself over his failure at Flahgens Peake. 'What do I do now?' he asked himself gloomily. 'Try again? Well, I could give it another try I suppose.' He sat there shivering in the cold, damp air, remembering the shadowy movements within the silver halo of his spell, and recalling the rotten stench of decay that had assailed his senses as he had cast the spell.

After brooding at some length, the realisation of what really had occurred hit him like a sledgehammer. 'Bogwights!' he spat. 'It just has to be! So – the spell did work after all.'

Rookwort then returned once more to his previous dark thoughts, as he pondered on two questions.

Had the Bogwights gained access into the mountain?

And if so, had they located the artefacts and fabled spell-books of Pangloria?

~ CHAPTER FIVE ~

Flitter's Tale

Flitter Trott was sitting on the floor in front of the four children, while Bouncer lay curled up with his head resting on Lorna's lap.

The children were all staring intently at the small figure of the wood sprite as he explained about himself and his relationship with the Damsel, Old Zeke and the Maiden.

'The Damsel,' he told them, 'is the most powerful being in the world of faerie, and is a spirit of the cosmos itself. She is what humans refer to as Mother Nature,' he said, looking at each of the children in turn, making sure that they understood all that he had told them.

'What does the Damsel look like?' Lorna asked. 'I mean, is she pretty?'

'Hmm,' replied Flitter Trott thoughtfully, 'no one has really seen her in her true form. She can appear differently to all creatures, maybe as some species of animal to some creatures, or as a woman clad simply in white to humans. But it is her spirit of *being* that is important, do you see? How she appears to you is between you and her. It is *that* special! As a matter of fact, I have only ever seen her once.'

'How did she appear to you, Flit?' Katie asked softly.

'Well,' he replied thoughtfully, 'she looked a lot like my mother. Does that surprise you all? Even I had a mother, you know. Now, if she appeared to one of *you* for instance, she may look like your aunt or your grandmother. As I've told you, it's different for each person or creature. Now, Ezekiel is one of three guardians sent over from Pangloria to help to take care of Badger Wood, and that is *no* small task, I can tell you! Ezekiel always was the Damsel's favourite and was a very powerful wizard when he was young man. That's why the Damsel chose him, but I'm afraid *that* didn't go down too well with his younger brother, Rookwort.'

Katie looked at the sprite in astonishment and asked, 'Wait a minute, Flit! Do you mean to *tell* me that Uncle Ezekiel has a brother?'

Flitter Trott nodded slowly. 'Why, yes. Hasn't Ezekiel ever told you?'

'No!' replied Katie quietly. 'No, never – I wonder why?'

'Flit, you've mentioned someone called the Maiden once or twice; who is she?' Barney asked politely.

'The Maiden, yes,' replied Flitter Trott, pausing to think for a moment. 'The Maiden is an exceptionally powerful white witch, who like Ezekiel and me was specially chosen by the Damsel herself to look after several of the Earth's havens and to watch over the Earth's inhabitants and its environment. You have to bear in mind that your world has recently survived the horrors of a world war, two in fact, and all that mankind could throw at it, and now there is a lot of healing which needs to take place. The Maiden is human of course,' he added as he caught the surprised expression reflected in their faces.

'The identity of the Maiden has to remain a secret, you see; here on Earth, humankind does not have a very good record with witches. They have always regarded them selfish and wicked, which of course isn't always true.'

Flitter Trott then went on to explain about the missing Foundling, what she meant to the creatures of Badger Wood, and what she meant to the land as a whole, although only a tiny number of people knew that such magical creatures even existed.

He paused for a few moments, while he collected his thoughts and after what seemed like an age added, 'You see, my young friends, Badger Wood is a haven where some of the ravages of mankind are kept at bay. There are of course a large number of similar havens throughout this world, each one having a different name and appearance.'

Flitter Trott moved his hands expressively, as he explained, 'For example, in the Sahara Desert, a haven may be an oasis, or in South America, a jungle hidden deep within a rain forest. But each haven will protect that region.'

'Does each haven have its own Foundling?' Lorna asked.

'Yes they do,' Flit replied, with a smile. 'But each

one is a very different species; one may be a monkey, a rat, or even a snake!

He grinned as he saw Barney shudder. 'Each Foundling is imbibed with nature's magic and is always female and pure white in colour. I suppose you could say that each Foundling is a sort of living, magic charm, and as each Foundling grows older it dies and is reborn in a different form; that way the magic survives and continues to protect the land.'

'What would happen if a Foundling was killed? Say, by hunters or by accident?' asked Barney seriously.

Flitter Trott stared hard at Barney through his jet black eyes for a moment, and replied, 'After a short time it would be reborn and the haven would continue. But if a Foundling is taken and its magic is drained from it, then the haven that it protects will fail and eventually die. The Black Wilt would set in and spread its sickness across the land. That is why the creatures of each haven protect their own Foundling. It's a sort of partnership – they protect the Foundling, and in turn the Foundling protects them and the land, and so the cycle of life continues.'

'What will happen here, Flit, if you can't find the Foundling?' Lenny asked.

Flitter Trott looked at them all, and they saw a deep sadness reflected in his dark eyes. 'If that should happen, Lenny, then I have failed as a guardian and the wood will simply die.

He sighed deeply and continued, 'The signs are already here, some of the trees already have the Black Wilt on their leaves and that is due to the Foundling being missing, that is why you children simply have to help me.'

'Flit,' whispered a gentle voice, and the sprite

looked up to see Katie kneeling in front of him with tears in her eyes. 'It's not *your* fault, you know; this is why my uncle sent me along with Barney and the twins to help if we can. You must be aware of this? After all, you've been watching Barney and the twins for years now, and you know how brave and resourceful they are. My uncle also knew this, and that is the reason why Barney was given the bedstead. Uncle Ezekiel also knew that the twins and Barney are very loyal friends and even asked them to become *my* friends so that we could travel to wherever the Foundling is and rescue her.'

Flitter Trott nodded as he gave them all a tight lipped smile and slowly his mind went through the events which led him to discover that the Foundling had been taken.

It suddenly dawned on him that there had been a lingering smell of rotting flesh which had been around the badger sett and around the Mound, the huge grass covered hill within the heart of Badger Wood. Flitter Trott had tried to track the Foundling's abductors, but couldn't find any trail, not even the old fox, Firebrand, could pick up any signs.

Slowly, he pieced together the tiny bits of information until he arrived at what he thought was the answer. 'Why, how stupid of me!' he suddenly exclaimed. 'Of course it's Bogwights that are behind all of this!'

'Excuse me, Flit, but why are you stupid? And what are Bogwights?' Barney asked.

Flitter Trott jumped up and began to pace up and down as he stroked his pointed beard thoughtfully. He turned suddenly, and looking at the children announced, 'I need you to go to Pangloria, as soon as you can, before it's too late.'

Why? Why do we need to go *there*?' Lorna asked giving Flit a look of panic.

Flitter Trott turned towards her and with a grim laugh replied, 'Because, my young friends, there's no one else, only *you*. I have to stay here of course and do what I can for the creatures of the wood. Ezekiel, as Katie has already said, is much too old for the task, and the Maiden will simply not go to Pangloria unless she absolutely has to; that leaves only *you*!' He jabbed a spindly finger in their direction to emphasise the point.

The children stared at one another in surprise; even Bouncer gave Flitter Trott a puzzled look as he cocked his shaggy head to one side.

Flitter Trott stepped over to Barney and placing both of his small hands on Barney's shoulders, said to him, 'As Katie has informed us, this is one of the reasons why you were given the bed-scapator. It can only be commanded by the person to whom it has been given.' Then prodding Barney in the chest with his finger he added, 'And that, my young friend, is *you*! I would consider it a great honour, Barney, and I have a notion that Ezekiel has seen something in you which reminded him of himself, when he was a boy.'

Barney looked at the sprite and in a determined voice asked, 'But how do I find Pangloria?'

With a quizzical look the sprite replied, 'Well, considering that you've already been there,' he paused, giving Barney a sly grin. 'Oh, don't look so surprised, Barney. I saw you last night, and a very funny sight it was too!'

Barney stared at the little man with a frown and asked, 'But Flit, how could you see me? When no one else in the village could?'

'Have you forgotten so soon that I am also a creature born out of natural magic, and I can see things that others can't – especially magic bedsteads! Now you listen up close, young Barney,' he said, prodding him once more in his chest. 'The portal into Pangloria is through that hill which you tried to crash into last night, only we call it the Mound.' Flitter Trott continued almost in a whisper, 'The only way in and out of Pangloria in these parts, is through Badger Wood and the Mound. And the only way through the Mound, is by using your bedstead or by using very powerful magic.'

He looked around at the others, and warned, 'Now I reckon that's how the Foundling was taken. Somehow the portal has been opened which has allowed the Bogwights to enter this world and take her, and believe me, you *do not* want any Bogwights coming into this world!'

Katie nodded and said, 'My uncle half suspected as much, and that's what drove him to make sure that Barney got the bed-scapator. Sorry, Barney,' she grimaced as she noticed the look of shock on his face, 'but I'm afraid Uncle Zeke was also responsible for your old bed collapsing and he needed someone who can travel in and out of Pangloria, particularly if I am away at boarding school and cannot be around.'

Flitter Trott placed his hands on his hips and burst out laughing, 'Ha, ha, ha, ha, Ezekiel always did have a sense of humour as well as style. Well, *all* is revealed at last.'

'Except that we still don't know what Bogwights actually are,' Lenny mused.

'Hmm,' the sprite replied. 'No, you don't, do you? And I'm not sure that you'd be any better off knowing, but since you're going to have to know sooner or later, I'll tell you – but listen very carefully,' he warned, 'and I mean *all* of you, Bogwights are downright dangerous creatures! There is nothing much that frightens them, and they are a match for anything that goes on four legs or even two legs for that matter!' He paused to make sure that the children were all listening. 'Bogwights are nasty creatures and are about as evil as they come, they are a sort of cross between a Wight and a Goblin, and have been the sworn enemies of wood sprites for thousands of years. It's because they covet our magic. In fact, they will go to *any* lengths to get magic, because they think that it will give them power over others.'

'But Flit, how do you know for sure that they took the Foundling?' asked Katie.

Flitter Trott shrugged his shoulders and replied, 'Well, I can't be absolutely certain.' He explained to the children about not being able to find any tracks, other than those of badgers, and the strong smell of decay he had found at the Foundling's sett and at the Mound.

He also told them how he had asked both Bouncer and Firebrand the fox to scour the wood time and time again, and they still couldn't find any tracks.

'If Bouncer and Firebrand couldn't find tracks then there aren't any,' he stated positively. 'What with no tracks and that rotten smell, it just has to be Bogwights. Somehow they must have found a way to open up the magic portal, stolen the Foundling and made their way back again; otherwise, if they were still here, the other guardians and I would have sensed them by now.'

'What will the Bogwights do to the Foundling, if they *have* got her?' asked Barney.

Flitter Trott gazed at them all and with a shake of his head he replied, 'It's most likely that they will try to leach her magic from her, or maybe even offer the Foundling up for some form of sacrifice. That's why it's important for you to get to Pangloria right away.' He paused for a moment and stroked his beard, as he mumbled to himself, 'But where to start, I wonder?'

After a moment, his dark eyes lit up and with a sly grin, he exclaimed, 'When you get there, you'll need to find Rookwort Crumpshaw!'

~ CHAPTER SIX ~

Pangloria

'Rookwort Crumpshaw!' Katie exclaimed. 'Is he related to my uncle, by any chance?'

'Umm – yes, as a matter of fact he is,' replied Flitter Trott almost guiltily.

'But how can he help us, Flit?' asked Barney. 'Could this Rookwort destroy these… Bogwights?'

'I don't know about that,' replied the wood sprite, 'but if anyone knows all there is to know about Bogwights, it's old Rookwort.'

Flitter Trott paced up and down for a while, then turning round he stared directly at Katie, who was now looking extremely puzzled, and said, 'I think that I'd better explain a few things about Rookwort. First and foremost, he is one of the Bogwights' most dangerous enemies.' The sprite stopped and gave them all a wry smile before continuing. 'Rookwort has not always been the best of spell casters and a long, long time ago, he used some of his magic upon a few Bogwights. He thought that he was helping them of course, but all that they were really after was his magic.' Flitter Trott paused for a second and snorted, 'the upshot of it was that his spell went badly wrong and a few Bogwights were destroyed. One or two of them at least were turned into large chunks of stone and a good thing too, if you want my opinion,' Flitter Trott continued with a grim smile. 'Goodness knows what chaos the Bogwights would have caused if they suddenly had any form of innate magic at their fingertips. Now, as for Rookwort, Katie, all I can tell you is that he happens to be your uncle's younger brother.'

'That's really odd,' Katie mused, 'because Uncle Ezekiel has never ever mentioned him – well not to me anyhow.'

Flitter Trott gave Katie a swift glance and shrugging his shoulders replied, 'I can't give you an answer to that, Katie, only to say that Ezekiel probably has his own reasons for not telling you about his brother.'

Katie nodded and asked, 'Does Rookwort look like my uncle?'

'Does he look like Ezekiel?' replied Flitter Trott with a laugh. 'Why, they're like two peas in a pod, except that Rookwort can be really grumpy, and he isn't *quite* the wizard that his brother is. Mind you, that's only because he's always felt overshadowed by Ezekiel. I happen to think that if he really wanted to, Rookwort could be one of the greatest wizards that Pangloria has ever seen.'

The three children gazed at Flitter Trott as he was speaking, totally absorbed in his description of

Rookwort. Then giving the sprite an intense stare, Katie asked, 'Flit, why didn't Rookwort come over to Plummington with Uncle Ezekiel?'

Flitter Trott grimaced and replied, 'He was envious.'

'What? Do you mean that he was jealous of my uncle?' Katie asked, sounding rather surprised.

'Yes,' Flit answered, 'I suppose I do, in a way. You see, Ezekiel had always been a better spell-caster than his brother, but that was only because Rookwort never had Ezekiel's confidence. That doesn't mean that Ezekiel didn't *try* to encourage him, in fact, I think that deep down Ezekiel always knew his younger brother had the makings of a truly great wizard.' Flitter Trott paused to ponder for a few moments before continuing, 'The problem that Rookwort had, was that he became angry and felt betrayed when the Damsel chose Ezekiel and the Maiden to become Earth's guardians. This meant that he would have to leave Pangloria and Rookwort.'

'So they *hate* each other now, I suppose?' Lorna commented.

'No, I don't think that they do,' replied Flitter Trott thoughtfully. 'I think Rookwort felt that Ezekiel, who – don't forget – was also his teacher, had left him alone, and he didn't really have anyone else to turn to. This of course left him feeling very bitter and mistrustful of others.'

'How do you know that Rookwort will trust us?' asked Lenny.

'The simple answer is that I don't,' Flitter Trott replied. 'But, as I've already said, you are all that I've got at the moment, and Rookwort has never really had any dealings with children. I honestly think that you might just be able to get him to help you, where others may not – and after all, blood is thicker than water, so they say. I have a notion that old Rookwort may even be pleased to find that he now has other relatives.'

Katie felt everyone's eyes fixed on her, as Flitter Trott's revelation sank in!

'Okay,' said Barney as he nodded his head, 'where can we find him?'

Flitter Trott pursed his lips and replied, 'I think that the Valley of the Fiery Holes is a good place to start. Rookwort tends to hang around in lonely places and you'll not find a lonelier place than that.'

He walked over to a large wooden chest of drawers situated in the corner of the room, and opening one of the many drawers, took out a small scroll of old, brown parchment.

Carefully unrolling it on the floor, he beckoned the children to come and look then said, 'This is a map which shows some parts of Pangloria. There are other maps showing a little more detail, but this will do you for now.'

They stared down at the small piece of parchment and saw that the map was well marked and clearly showed a group of mountains, a large area of marsh land, and a desolate area called the Wormwood Wastes. They could also see an area of woodland and a shoreline, leading to a large expanse of water marked as the Goranan Sea.

Flitter Trott's tiny hands flew over the map as he pointed out its various features. He paused for a moment, to check that they were all paying attention and warned, 'When you get there, try to keep in and around the Stag Mountains, and *do not* enter the area called the Rotten Marshes after dark! You never know what's lurking around there at night.

Pausing for a moment, he wagged his finger at them and added, 'Remember! You have been warned! Try to get to the Valley of the Fiery Holes during daylight; although, I don't think that any Bogwights will bother going in there unless they really have to, they're not overly fond of fire. But you can't be too careful.'

Barney's face expressed concern as he asked Flitter Trott, 'How am I going to explain to my mum about all of this? She's bound to notice that I'm missing.'

'So will our mum and dad,' echoed the twins.

Flitter Trott had a highly amused look on his face and noticed that Katie gave Barney and the Barker twins a knowing sort of smile. 'Still haven't worked it out, have you, boy?' replied Flitter Trott with a laugh. 'Your bedstead is not affected by time! So if you leave for Pangloria at say, five o'clock, when you return, it will still *be* five o'clock!'

The twins and Barney looked at Flitter Trott incredulously, and Barney asked, 'So my mum would *never* be any the wiser?'

'No,' said Flitter Trott. 'Not a chance, unless she *actually* sees you disappear for a second or two. So you'll just have to be careful that she doesn't see you, Barney, won't you? Now!' he shouted suddenly, clapping his hands. 'I think that you should begin your journey as soon as you can. The bed-scapator should carry you all easily enough – and I would take Bouncer along with you, I reckon that he will prove to be pretty useful.'

The children nodded excitedly as Flitter Trott continued, 'You're going to need some sort of ruse to get all of you into Barney's bedroom though, particularly in broad daylight.'

They all sat in silence for several long minutes as the tiny little cuckoo clock, which hung on the wall in front of them, ticked away loudly. After what seemed like an age, Barney suddenly yelled, 'Listen! I think I've got a plan,' and carefully began to explain his idea...

Next morning, as Barney was lying in bed wide awake, thinking about the forthcoming journey into Pangloria, he heard the familiar voice of his mum calling from the bottom of the staircase. 'Barney, come on, son, you need to get a move on – it's time that you were up, your breakfast's on the table.'

Barney lay there, quietly, just as he had planned, and before long he heard his mother's feet, stomping up the stairs, mumbling something about him being a 'lazy little devil'. Suddenly his bedroom door opened and his mum bustled in as she scolded him, 'Come on, lazy bones, it really is time that you were up.'

'Aw, I'm sorry, Mum, but I don't feel very well at all,' Barney replied as he gave Olivia a sickly look. 'I've got an awful headache and I feel really ill!'

His mum's face softened as she put her hand upon his brow and said, 'Oh you poor dear, I bet that you're coming down with something.' She ordered him to stick out his tongue and examined it closely. 'Hmm, I tell you what, Barney, you can have your breakfast in bed and lie-in for a while, and if you're no better later on today I'll get Doctor Grice to pop in, how about that?'

Barney nodded weakly and Olivia disappeared back down the stairs to collect his breakfast.

After Barney had finished his meal, his mother came in again and with a look of surprise she murmured, 'Well, young man, you soon polished your breakfast off, whatever it is that's wrong with you, it certainly hasn't affected your appetite has it?'

'I don't feel quite so sick now, Mum, but my head still aches and all of my bones hurt,' Barney answered, with a slight note of panic in his voice.

'Hmm,' replied his mum as she narrowed her eyes in suspicion. 'We'll see how you are this afternoon.' A moment later they heard a sharp knock on the front door. 'I wonder who that could be,' Olivia wondered out loud.

'It might be Lorna and Lenny, Mum – I'm supposed to be meeting them at their cottage.'

Olivia disappeared downstairs to answer the door. Barney thought to himself that everything was going to plan quite nicely.

After a few moments his bedroom door opened and in trooped Katie, the twins and Bouncer, who was wagging his tail happily.

'Visitors to see you, Barney,' announced his mum with a smile. 'I've told them that you weren't feeling very well, but they still wanted to come up and see you.'

'Yeah,' added Lenny giving Barney a sly wink, 'but that's only if you're feeling up to it? Mind you, I don't think that you look at all well.' Barney desperately tried to smother a laugh by pretending to have a fit of coughing!

'I think that's very kind of them, don't you, dear?' said Barney's mum, appearing not to have noticed Barney's cover up.

Barney nodded, barely able to keep the excitement from showing on his face; the last thing that he wanted now was to give the game away at this stage. His mum was still smiling and announced, 'Now, I've just got to pop out for an hour or so to see Mrs Bhylls about her washing and to have a chat, so don't tire Barney too much, will you, my dears?'

'No we won't, Mrs Betts,' Lorna replied sweetly, 'we'll take good care of him, we promise.'

'Why, thank you, Lorna dear, you really are very kind. It's lovely for Barney to have such nice friends.' After pausing for a moment Olivia asked, 'And you, my dear – I'm sorry but have we met before? Only I can't seem to remember your name.'

'Oh, I'm Katie, umm – Katie Crabtree,' replied Katie in her dreamy voice. 'I haven't known Barney or the twins for very long – but I believe that you know my uncle Zeke?'

'Oh do you mean that nice old gentleman from Crumpshaw's Emporium? Is he really your uncle?' Barney's mum asked, with a look of surprise.

Katie nodded and went on to explain to Olivia that she always stayed with her uncle over the school holidays, and then told her how she met Barney and the twins.

Olivia listened to the dreamy-looking girl who stood in front of her, and then announced suddenly, 'Well! I *can't* hang around here all day; I've people to see and things to do! Now I'm only going to be gone for a couple of hours, Barney, and you shouldn't be needing anything while I'm out, and besides, you've got your friends for company.'

With that, Olivia gave them all a tiny wave and headed out of the bedroom and back down the stairs. After a few minutes the children heard Olivia go out of the front door and shout, 'I won't be long, Barney.'

'Okay Mum,' he replied, giving Katie and the twins a triumphant grin. Lenny took a sneaky peek out of the bedroom window and watched Barney's mum as she disappeared down Cat and Kittens Lane. Then turning to the others he said, 'Okay, the coast is clear.'

'Great!' Barney replied excitedly, and then asked Lorna and Lenny, 'Have you both got your catapults and ammo?'

'Of course we have,' Lorna retorted, 'mind you, we've run out of those old marbles; have you got any left?'

'Not many,' Barney replied with a frown.

'Well, it's too late to do anything about it now,' Lenny muttered. 'I guess that we'll just have to use the new ones that we bought from Katie, but only if we have to. Oh!' he added with a grin, 'I've borrowed Dad's torch too, just in case we need it.'

'Well, I'd say that we're set to go, then,' said Katie, staring at Barney and the twins. 'So if you hurry up and get dressed, Barney, we can be on our way.'

'Ooh, she's keen isn't she?' said Lenny with a smirk, totally missing the look of warning that Lorna had given him.

Katie and the twins left the bedroom for a few moments, while Barney quickly got dressed, and very soon they heard his voice call out, 'Okay I'm ready!'
The four children climbed up carefully onto the large bedstead, with Bouncer sitting between Katie and Lorna. They all glanced at one another nervously as Barney took a deep breath and whispered, 'Well, here goes.' Then in a louder voice he gave the command, 'To bed and away!'

The children all let out a loud gasp of amazement as they saw the whole of the wall in front of them simply melt away!

Bouncer gave a small yelp as the bedstead suddenly leapt forward and moved smoothly into Cat and Kittens Lane, before it suddenly shot like a rocket, high into the sky above.

'Whoopee!' shouted Lenny and Barney as the bedstead climbed higher and higher, into a very thin layer of cloud. Barney grinned at them all and cried, 'Bed! Please stop!'

The bedstead slowed and came to a stop, high above Plummington Minor which now looked like a tiny model village, far below. Barney turned to Katie and Lorna and saw that they were gripping the sides of the bedstead tightly, their knuckles almost white with the effort of stooping themselves from tumbling back to the ground, far below.

Barney gave them a beaming smile, as he said, 'Look, just relax and enjoy the ride; the bedstead won't let you fall, it's probably part of its magic to keep us safe.'

'What now?' Lenny asked, staring all around him excitedly.

'We go to Pangloria, of course!' Katie replied nervously. 'But I'm not looking forward to the ride.'

Barney turned to them all and shouted, 'Listen everyone, when we head back down to the ground it will seem like we're going to crash.' As he saw the look of fear creep into their eyes, he quickly reassured them, 'But just trust me, we're going to be fine.'

He turned and cried, 'Bed! Please take us into Pangloria, now!'

Without any warning, the bedstead plummeted in a steep arc through the dark clouds that surrounded Badger Wood.

Lorna squealed in fear and Bouncer was barking and howling as they saw the trees within the wood looming ever closer.

Falling and faster, the large bedstead hurtled towards the dark interior of Badger Wood. They suddenly caught sight of the Mound, and closed their eyes tightly, as they plummeted at breakneck speed towards it!

Howling with delight, Barney heard the now familiar whooshing sound as the bedstead appeared to crash into the side of the grassy hill! In an instant, the bed had levelled out and they were now flying over a large range of mountains.

Barney laughed and yelled over his shoulder, 'It's okay. You can all open your eyes now. We've arrived.'

'Crikey, is this Pangloria?' Lenny asked, blinking in disbelief.

'It sure is,' replied Barney. 'We're above the Stag Mountains, if I'm not mistaken.'

Katie had unravelled the little roll of parchment, which Flitter Trott had given her, and after studying it for a few moments she asked, 'Barney, can you see that large area of scrubland over there, to your left?'

'Yes, I think so,' he replied, his eyes squinting in the poor light of the Panglorian night sky.

'Well, head for that if you can, we can wait around there until dawn,' Katie suggested, still studying the map. 'It should be much lighter then, and it will give us time to get our bearings.'

'How do you know where we need to head for, Katie?' asked Lorna.

'Flit told me what to look for when he gave me this map,' Katie replied. 'He thought that Barney would have enough to do, with flying the bed-scapator.'

'Just where is it that we're heading for?' Barney asked, shouting over his shoulder to Katie.

'As far as I can make out, we need to head for a place called the Wormwood Wastes,' Katie replied. 'Flit told me that if we had to wait until daylight, then it would be the safest place.'

Barney flew the bedstead according to Katie's directions and headed towards the Wormwood Wastes. The bedstead flew on for a while until they were just outside the range of the Stag Mountains when Katie suddenly shouted, 'Here will do fine.'

Barney nodded and shouted, 'Bed! Please stop and land.' Immediately, the bedstead slowed down and landed smoothly on an area of scrub grass.

The children carefully looked around them in the dim light of dawn and saw the dark line of what appeared to be woodland on the far horizon. 'That must be Fligget Wood,' Katie informed them as she continued poring over the small brown map, 'so we must be somewhere close to the north-west end of the mountains.'

'Do you think that we'll be okay to step down and stretch our legs for a while?' Lorna asked. 'I mean, the bed won't fly away or anything, will it?'

'No I don't think so,' replied Katie. 'The bed-scapator will only obey the command of the person who it belongs to, and that's Barney, so it should be quite safe.'

Warily, the children stepped down and began to walk around a little, being careful not to stray too far from their only means of transport out of Pangloria. Bouncer began running round, happily barking and wagging his tail.

'Bouncer, be quiet,' commanded Lenny. 'You might attract attention to us.'

'What! Way out here?' Katie giggled. 'I don't think so; there isn't anything else for miles. No, we're quite safe; *really*, we can hang around here for as long as we need to.'

'Don't tell me! You've been here already,' taunted

Lenny.

Katie just pulled a face at him, bobbed out her tongue and replied with a huff, 'As it happens, *no* I haven't.'

'Oh Katie, don't take any notice of him, he's always teasing,' Lorna chided, as she glared at Lenny. 'He's just jealous because you know some things that *he* doesn't, but then, that's *boys* for you.'

Barney and Lenny simply rolled their eyes and tutted, giving each other 'here we go again' looks.

After hanging around the edge of the Wormwood Wastes for a an hour or so Barney said, 'Well I suppose we'd better have a look at that map again, if we want to plan the next part of our journey. It's getting lighter already and should be fully light soon.'

They all crowded round the map and saw that the Valley of the Fiery Holes lay towards the southern end of the Stag Mountains.

'I tell you what,' suggested Lorna, 'why don't we get moving now, and if we don't find anything, we can still get back here before it gets dark.' The others saw the sense in her suggestion and nodded in agreement.

'How are we going to keep track of the time?' Barney asked.

'Dead easy,' Lenny replied proudly, flashing the shiny, silver watch on his wrist. I've got my uncle Arthur's old army watch that he gave me last year, and it's a real good one too, it never loses a second.'

Within a quarter of an hour the children noticed that it was light enough to continue their journey, and they all climbed back onto the bed-scapator.

Barney shouted the words, 'Bed! Please take us to the Stag Mountains,' and the bedstead lifted itself smoothly into the air. Barney leaned forwards and to one side a little, bringing the bedstead round in a smooth arc to head south at a steady speed back towards the Stag Mountains.

Before the children knew it, they were flying once more above the snow-capped mountain range and could clearly see the largest mountain, Flahgens Peake, which Katie identified from the map.

She tapped Barney on his shoulder and said, 'Head for the highest mountain, the one that has a lot of snow on its tip.' Barney nodded and adjusted his direction slightly.

'The Valley of the Fiery Holes is just below the base of Flahgens Peake,' she informed Barney as she pointed to the valley's position on the map.

As the morning sky was fairly clear around the range of mountains, the children could see for many miles. They saw small herds of mountain goats and wild deer moving around the various valleys and peaks of the mountains. They also caught a glimpse of a very large area of inhospitable marshland which was shrouded here and there by a forbidding dense mist.

'That must be the Rotten Marshes that Flit warned us about,' shouted Katie to the others.

'Yeah, and that's where the Bogwights could be holed up,' Lenny replied, grimly. 'I remember Flit telling me yesterday that they like to live deep down under any large rocky ruins or the remains of ancient fortresses. He reckoned that one old fortress lies somewhere in the middle of those marshes.'

They flew through the mountain range and saw all manner of creatures either hunting prey, or more timid creatures that were trying to hide from predators. None of the creatures seemed to be aware of the children or the bedstead, as it flew above them.

After flying around for a while, they spotted the Valley of the Fiery Holes before them and decided to fly in a large descending circle around its edge in order to check out the lay of the land.

The valley looked as though it had been hewn out of a gigantic lump of grey rock, and at its southern end they could see the three large fiery holes which appeared like the red, gaping scars of three gigantic wounds. As they flew nearer they saw occasional jets of fiery larva as they erupted high into the air.

They circled again and decided to land at the northern end of the valley, well away from the dangerous-looking eruptions. They flew towards the northern end and Lenny suddenly shouted to the others, 'What's that down there, to our right, can you see that old cabin? It looks like someone could be living there!'

As they neared the northern end of the valley, Barney yelled, 'Bed! Please stop and land here.' The bed instantly slowed down, and halted, then after hovering for a moment, landed gently upon the ash covered ground.

The children climbed down from the bedstead and stood silently looking at the terrain that lay around them. 'This place is a bit miserable isn't it?' Lorna moaned, wrinkling her nose distastefully. 'Even Bouncer doesn't want to explore it!' she added, as Bouncer stood silently by her side, staring about him warily.

'Well, let's have a look around,' Lenny suggested, 'but remember that we must all keep together.'

They all began to walk towards the southern end of the valley, kicking up little clouds of volcanic dust as they went. After a while they spotted the old cabin that

Lenny had seen earlier in the distance. As they continued to walk towards the solitary cabin, they began to notice how lonely the valley made them feel and a deep sense of unease began to surround them all.

They continued to walk on stoically however, with a sense of grim determination, and after a while they spotted that the old cabin now appeared to be much closer and began to hurry towards it.

As they got to within three hundred yards of the cabin, Bouncer suddenly gave a low growl of warning, and stepped out protectively in front of the four children.

In that instant the ground in front of Bouncer began to move and a huge figure, which appeared to be made of wet clay and ash, rose up menacingly from out of the ground and began to move slowly and silently towards them!

~ CHAPTER SEVEN ~

Rookwort's Folly

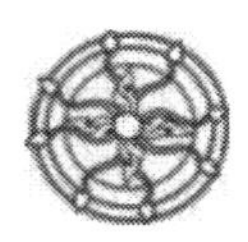

Deep in the heart of Badger Wood, three young men were moving silently along the narrow path that ran alongside Dingle Brook. The clinking sound of their small steel traps cut through the brooding silence as they rattled loosely on the shoulders of the poachers. Although they tried to step carefully as they entered the darkness of the wood, one of them tripped and made an awful racket, causing a startled crow to fly away noisily.

'Keep yer noise down, can't yer, ya clumsy idiots,' snarled Jed Hopwood as he turned to give the other two young men a nasty look. 'D'yer want ter give the game away?'

'Aw, you keep your noise down, Jed Hopwood,' roared Ginger Smollett. 'You're always moaning at somebody else, when half the time it's *you* that's making all the noise.'

Jed cursed and spat as they all stumbled along the path. The other two young men simply shook their heads in disbelief and plodded on, the metal traps which hung heavily on their shoulders, still clinking loudly.

After a few hundred yards they waded across a shallow part of Dingle Brook and the two young men began to curse Jed loudly as the water poured in over the tops of their boots. Finally, after what seemed to be hours of struggling through the rough terrain of brambles and long, reed-like grass, they reached the heart of Badger Wood, fairly close to the Mound.

Jed sat down heavily on a large oak branch which had fallen during the recent storm, trying to empty his water filled boots.

The third poacher, Gilbert Smollett, looked around the wood uneasily and whispered, 'You know what, lads, I keep getting the feeling that we're being watched; it ain't half creepy in here.'

'What's the matter, lickle Gilly?' Jed snorted nastily. 'Frightened of the nasty old Bogey Man are yer?'

Ginger moved over to Jed and glaring fiercely, warned him, 'Hey Hopwood! You leave our Gil alone or else!'

'Or else you'll do *what*? Yer great big sissy,' Jed sneered.

Ginger gave Jed a steely-eyed stare and stepping right up to him, shook a large, hard fist in his Jed's pallid face, and through his gritted teeth, snarled menacingly, 'Or else I'm going to flatten that great *stupid* nose of yours, and fill that oversized gob with this here! And I'll do it good and proper *see*! You've been at our Gil for ages now, so you'd better leave him be from now on, or you'll have me to reckon with. Do you understand, Hopwood?'

Jed, as usual when tackled by anyone his own size or anyone who stood up to him, crumpled like a pack of cards. His face instantly became paler, and he nodded meekly, and mumbled something that sounded like, 'Only joking.'

Ginger glared at him balefully as he grunted with satisfaction, 'Right! Now *that's* sorted, let's get these traps set! It'll be dark soon.'

Jed and the Smollett brothers worked quietly and before long had laid several of the cruel looking traps along the various animal tracks which criss-crossed the undergrowth within Badger Wood.

'What sort of catch do you reckon we'll get, Jed?' Gilbert asked. 'Only we normally use these traps to catch rabbits and the like, on our farm.'

Jed gave him a sidelong glance and replied sulkily, 'Anything that comes along I suppose, but I hope it's that great big, flea-bitten wolf of the Barkers – the cocky little gits, it'll serve 'em right!'

Ginger just glared at him once more and shook his head, as he sneered, 'Yeah, that's about your barrow isn't it, Hopwood? You know what I mean – *little* kids. I don't know if we'd bother with you at all, if wasn't for the chance of a little sport, would we Gil?'

Gil shook his head and gave Jed a look of pure loathing.

After an hour of careful preparation, all of the traps were baited and set. Markers made from pieces of broken branches and twigs had been carefully left sticking up from the dense undergrowth to show the poachers where each of the traps was located, as they planned to return the next day, sometime around dawn, to retrieve their quarry. The three men, now satisfied with their ghastly preparations, made their way out of the wood, trampling down the undergrowth as they went.

Jed and the Smollett brothers hadn't noticed the two figures which stood way back within the darkness of the trees, watching them as they made their way back home.

Both pairs of sapphire blue and jet black eyes were blazing with anger as they watched the backs of the poachers disappear out of Badger Wood.

Flitter Trott and the slender figure of the Maiden both shook their heads as the three men finally disappeared out of sight, before Flitter Trott asked, 'What do we do now, Ma'am? Should we send for Ezekiel?'

The Maiden paced up and down for a few moments, frowning as she decided. Then she replied, 'No, Flit. I don't think that we need to involve Ezekiel at this point. I think that we can deal with these young men ourselves. Besides, he has enough to worry about with the Foundling going missing. I think that our best course of action is to play these devils at their own game.'

Calling Flitter Trott to come closer, the Maiden began to explain what she had in mind...

The four children stood rooted to the spot as they stared up at the gigantic form which towered above them. Barney and the twins quickly drew their catapults, but began to fumble nervously as they loaded them with their marbles.

Katie yelled, 'Run for it!' as the mud-like creature

slowly advanced towards them. They backed away slowly, as the shambling creature continued to make its way silently towards them, reaching out to gather them all within its huge trunk-like arms.

Bouncer backed off a little at a time, his deep growls now become more and more menacing. Suddenly the creature moved quickly and lunged at Lorna, swinging its massive arms in a bear-like strike, barely missing her head.

The children scattered in a wide circle, with squeals and howls of fear. Bouncer quickly circled the giant creature, and then without any hesitation leapt up into the air to strike at the creature's throat.

As Bouncer crashed into the creature's gigantic body, it simply shuddered and quickly dissolved into a huge pile of slimy looking mud. The children gasped in surprise as they saw the mud quickly seep back into the ground!

Taking several deep breaths, they looked around them nervously, waiting for another attack, but saw no sign of anything or anyone in the valley except themselves.

Bouncer was busy sniffing and examining the ground closely as he tried to track the whereabouts of the mysterious creature.

'What on earth was that?' cried Lorna, still shaking from the encounter. 'I've never seen anything like that before – even in my worst nightmare.'

'Beats me,' Lenny replied grimly. 'I think that we're going to have to be *really* on our guard here, that thing could come back at any moment, and heaven knows what else is lurking around just waiting to attack us, so we need to be careful.'

Bouncer padded up to Lorna and rubbed his large

wolfish head against her body in reassurance, and then proceeded to lick her hands gently. 'Oh Bouncer,' she cried gratefully, 'I don't know what we'd have done without you. You saved us, you brave boy.' Bouncer gave her gentle 'woof' in reply.

'Well,' muttered Barney, 'we'd better get a move on just in case that creature does come back. But we're pretty close to that old cabin now. The sooner we find out who's living there the better.'

The children continued to walk slowly towards the old cabin and as they drew close to it they noticed that from the outside, it looked as if it was becoming run-down and sadly in need of some repair.

The cabin appeared to be built from large pine logs and had a grass covered roof from which sprouted a crooked chimney built from large grey stones. As they got closer they could see that the cabin had a single stout-looking door and a small boarded up window.

'Huh! I wonder who'd want to live in a dingy old dump like this?' said Lenny, wrinkling up his nose in apparent disgust.

'Well, it certainly won't be you, will it? You young jackanapes!' cried an angry voice. 'Do you always make rude remarks about other people's homes?'

And from the rear of the old cabin appeared the grumpiest looking old man that any of them had ever seen!

Dawn arrived gracefully over Badger Wood as the Maiden and Flitter Trott awaited the return of the three poachers. Before long they could hear the whisper of the gruff voices as the three poachers came noisily through the wood, trampling down the undergrowth recklessly in their eagerness to collect their prey.

The Maiden made a pass with her pale white hands and a haze of silver light leapt forward like a torch beam as it seared deeply into the wood ahead.

'That should distract them for a while, Flit,' she whispered to the wood sprite. 'Let's stay well-hidden and watch the fun, shall we?'

Jed, Ginger and Gilbert slowed down and moved more carefully as they began to encounter an area of thick brambles. 'What was that?' said Gilbert, as he looked around him nervously, seeing a bright flash of light.

'How d'ya expect me ter know, Gilly boy,' replied Jed impatiently. 'It's probably the animals that we've trapped, still trying ter get away, hah! They probably know what's going ter happen to 'em, don't they?'

They walked on for little while until Ginger stopped suddenly and exclaimed, 'Here we are, I remember that grass covered hill over there. Look! There's one of our markers, and another, and another.' He pointed to each of the markers in turn.

'Now remember what we agreed, we just neck 'em quick and pop 'em into the sack,' rasped Jed. 'And for gawd's sake don't forget to bring the traps back wiv ya!'

The three poachers split up and each man headed for one of the many markers. As they moved slowly forward, Jed suddenly let out a howl of pain and fell among the bracken and undergrowth, writhing in agony. The Smollett brothers grinned at each other as they heard Jed's cries for help, and both shaking their heads, started to move towards him.

Suddenly, down went Ginger with a loud squeal, as he cried out, 'Oh that hurts!'

Gilbert stopped dead in his tracks and shouted, 'Hey our Ginger, are you alright?'

'No I blooming well ain't,' squealed his brother. 'Get this thing off me!'

As Gilbert stepped forward to help his brother he felt the sudden pain of his ankle bone crack, as one of the spring-loaded traps snapped shut around his leg! He almost fainted with the pain as he fell and became dimly aware of Jed's snarling voice shouting, 'Somebody's moved all the traps about!'

After several long, excruciating minutes, the three panic-stricken poachers were hobbling as fast as they could out of Badger Wood. Their ankles were still firmly caught in the steel traps as they dragged them along through the undergrowth. The poachers' cries and whimpers could be heard long after they disappeared from view.

Flitter Trott and the Maiden stepped out from their hiding place and watched as the three young men disappeared, howling in pain, out of Badger Wood. 'Cruel, I know,' murmured Flitter Trott, 'but it had to be done.'

The previous evening the wood sprite had sent a message with old Firebrand the fox to all the creatures of Badger Wood, warning them of the danger. As a result none of the creatures had become ensnared.

The Maiden stepped forward, her blue eyes blazing triumphantly, and then with a wave of her hands she uttered the words, 'Steel-a-Melta.' For an instant, the remaining steel traps glowed brightly in the early morning light, then simply melted away, leaving no trace other than several tiny piles of ash in the undergrowth.

'Well, don't just *stand* there gawping at me,' shouted the old man rudely. '*Who* are you and *what* do you want?'

The three children stood dumbfounded, their mouths wide open in shocked surprise at the wrath of the angry old man. Barney thought that he looked remarkably like Old Zeke and was certain that this was the same old man that he had seen in his dream two nights ago.

Katie's eyes narrowed as she answered, 'You must be my uncle Rookwort. Flitter Trott said that you could be very grumpy *and* that you had no manners.'

'What do you mean, *uncle*?' The old man replied suspiciously. 'And how is it that you know that mischievous little sprite Flitter Trott? And as for my manners, well you've got a confounded cheek! Coming here, disturbing my peace and my rest!'

'It's rather a long story I'm afraid,' Katie replied, 'but if you've got a couple of hours to spare I suppose that we *could* explain it all to you.'

'If *I've* got a couple of hours to spare, *you* could explain!' the old man blustered. 'I'll tell you what *I* want, girl! I want *you* and your friends *gone*! This instant! And the way out is *back* the way you came!' he shouted angrily, pointing back down towards the northern end of the valley. 'I had thought that my mud-beast would have been more than enough to scare you away.'

'Mud-beast!' cried Lorna in shock. 'You mean to say that *you* set that foul creature against us?' She gave the old man a look of sheer contempt.

'Well, I only meant to scare you away,' the old man replied, now suddenly appearing quite sheepish and looking very guilty.

Lorna stepped forward with both hands on her hips, her eyes blazing with fierce indignation. 'Just trying to *scare* us away were you? Why you mean, *nasty*, cantankerous old man!' she roared, now losing all self-control. 'I was almost killed back there! If it hadn't been for Bouncer that mud-beast creature, or whatever you call that thing, would have had me there and then. You ought to be ashamed of yourself, you horrible sour-faced old man!'

Rookwort's face went purple with a mixture of rage and embarrassment as he replied, 'Now you just hold on a moment, young lady! I'm old enough to be *your* grandfather, and I will *not* be spoken to in that way, and another thing, I didn't *ask* you all to come rampaging into my valley!'

Then calming down a little he added sulkily, 'Besides, how was *I* to know that you were only children, you could have been anyone or *anything*, for all I knew.'

He paused for a moment or two and added, 'Anyway, the mud-beast was only a soil imp that I conjured up, and it wouldn't have harmed you – well not permanently.'

'Oh no, not unless you consider that it nearly scared us all to death,' replied Lorna still feeling angry.

Rookwort simply grunted in reply, and staring stonily at Katie snapped, 'Well young lady, you still haven't explained *who* you are and *what* you are doing here.'

Lenny smirked as he replied, 'That's because you were too busy calling us horrible names and setting nasty creatures on us to find out.'

'Huh! It's your own fault, creeping into a person's valley and trying to enter his home! I *suppose* you'd like me to say that I'm really sorry and make you all cups of tea and feed you while you tell me why you're here,' replied Rookwort, shaking his head in disbelief. 'Dratted children, you're all the same.'

'Well, it would be a much nicer introduction, wouldn't it,' Barney suggested with a rueful smile. Rookwort's craggy face softened a little and he nodded, as he appeared to be thinking Barney's suggestion over.

'Well, I owe you that much I suppose,' he admitted grudgingly. Then he nodded reluctantly and replied, 'Oh, come on then, but mind you don't touch anything, any of you! And make sure that dog of yours doesn't upset anything either!'

He turned sharply on his heels and headed back into his cabin. The children smiled and looked at each other in amazement, then shrugging their shoulders and shaking their heads they followed Rookwort inside.

They were very surprised to see that the inside of the cabin appeared to be far larger than the outside. There was an air of rough comfort about the old cabin, which gave it a nice warm homely feel. Rookwort allowed himself a ghost of a smile as he saw through a sideways glance that the children seemed to be impressed and at ease.

A welcoming fire was burning brightly in an old stone fireplace, above which hung a large black kettle that was boiling away merrily. Around the cabin stood row after row of shelves packed with jars of preserves, lots of dusty old books, and an array of ancient brass instruments which were humming and whirring, occasionally emitting a strange whistle or a tiny bang, as well as the occasional puff of brightly coloured smoke.

At one end of the cabin there stood a large wooden bed covered in several black furs and a large pink, fluffy pillow. Hanging from the rafters of the roof above the bed, was a number of smoked meats and sausages.

Barney also noticed a large map labelled 'Pangloria' hanging over the fireplace. It showed a far greater level of detail and more of Pangloria than the small parchment map that Fitter Trott had given them.

Rookwort gestured impatiently for the children to sit down on some wooden stools, which stood next to a table that looked as though it had been hewn from a single trunk of a large tree.

As the children sat down on each of the stools, Bouncer moved over to the fireplace and lay down in front of the cosy looking fire.

'Well?' Rookwort snapped, as he looked at each of the children in turn, and poured the tea into five rough clay mugs. I think that it's high time that you told me who you are, and why you are in my valley pestering me.'

Barney was about to answer when he felt Katie's hand squeeze his arm. 'I think that I should begin our tale!' she announced with a smile.

Rookwort listened in stony silence as Katie explained who they were, where they had come from and how she was related to him, she also explained what their purpose was in coming to find him.

At first Rookwort shook his head violently in disbelief, but as Katie continued to tell him about his brother Ezekiel and her mother Pandora, he looked up at her and she could see his piercing grey eyes beginning to become moistened.

It seemed very strange to Katie as she found herself thinking of how his eyes were almost identical to her uncle Ezekiel's, and how alike the two brothers were. She took her time to explain everything carefully, occasionally pausing to answer questions that Rookwort asked and getting either Barney or one of the twins to confirm that what she was saying was true.

Barney picked up his part of the tale. He explained

about his bed being broken and how he'd then obtained his magic bedstead. When he told Rookwort about his dreams and his first journey into Pangloria, he noticed a strange gleam appear in the old man's eyes.

Katie then explained about the missing Foundling and how Ezekiel, Flitter Trott, and the Maiden, who were the guardians of Badger Wood, had sent them to search for the Foundling.

Rookwort's keen eyes bored into hers intently as he listened and occasionally nodded his head. After Katie had finished a brooding silence descended upon the cabin as Rookwort seemed to be wrestling with his thoughts and emotions.

Suddenly he stood up and started to pace up and down the length of the cabin, his hands clasped behind his back, as he began mumbling to himself.

After what seemed like an age he sat down again and staring at them all intently, said, 'Now listen to me very carefully, all of you.' Then making certain that he had their undivided attention, he added, 'I think I know where the Foundling has been taken and why!'

Lorna went to say something, but Rookwort held up his hand and said firmly, 'Be quiet! I haven't finished. I have for some time been concerned about strange goings on within these mountains, but more so around the Rotten Marshes, and it wasn't until just now that I realised why I've been uneasy.'

Rookwort then explained about his recent quest for the fabled books of magic which he believed were held within the heart of Flahgens Peake. He told the children about how he had tried unsuccessfully to gain entrance into the mountain and how he couldn't figure out why he had failed, until now!

'I am now certain that the so called books of magic

were only a story put about by Bogwights to fool me into opening the portal within Flahgens Peake.' And through gritted teeth he added, 'And like an old fool, I fell for it, as a greedy bird falls for a juicy worm!'

He looked at the children and noting the shock that registered in their faces, continued, 'That's why I couldn't find the portal, because the shadow that I saw was in fact a Bogwight slipping past me into the portal, which enabled it to enter into your world. That's why I could smell their stench and that's why Flitter Trott could smell it too!'

'But how can you know that for certain?' asked Barney, sounding puzzled.

'Can't you see it, boy? It's the only explanation that makes sense,' he replied. 'The Bogwights have got the Foundling, believe me! And I guess that Flitter Trott is right, they will probably sacrifice her so they can leech her magic, and it's all through my own folly. Can't you see?' he croaked in a hoarse whisper, 'it's my fault!'

~ CHAPTER EIGHT ~

Pyton Cove

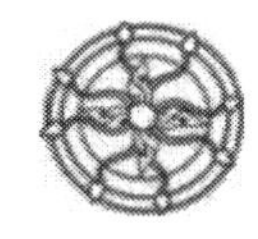

The children stared at Rookwort as if they had been struck dumb, even Bouncer sat up with a start and gazed at the old man intently. Katie looked around at the others as though she were looking for some form of agreement and said, 'Uncle Rook, why are you blaming yourself?'

The old man's face softened a little and in return he asked Katie, 'Girl, why are you calling me uncle?'

Katie gave him a sweet smile and replied, 'Well, you *are* my uncle even if you do belong in another world. Look, Uncle Rook, until recently I wasn't aware that you even existed. I always felt that Uncle Ezekiel was keeping something back, and he never spoke much about his life in Pangloria.'

Rookwort started to reply but Katie knelt in front

of him and placed her hands upon his and in a quiet, pleading voice begged, 'Please, Uncle, let me finish.'

Rookwort's mouth snapped shut and with a resigned shrug he continued to listen.

'I have always known that Uncle Ezekiel was special – you know, magical and all that. But he never really did explain how he came to Plummington or why he left Pangloria. Flitter Trott did that; he explained a lot of things and sort of filled in some of the gaps, if you know what I mean.' Katie paused for a moment then continued. 'There are some things that I'm still not sure about, such as how Uncle Ezekiel is *really* related to me. My mum used to say that he was her uncle, but she never explained properly about her mother and father, or her side of the family. I have always found that a bit strange.'

Rookwort looked searchingly into Katie's eyes and after a few moments, asked, 'Has Ezekiel ever mentioned anyone else – a woman, perhaps, who came with him from Pangloria?'

'No, I don't think so,' replied Katie. Then pausing to think for a moment she said, 'The only other people he ever mentioned were Flitter Trott and someone called the Maiden, but her identity has always been kept from me, even Flit wouldn't tell me who she is.'

'Hmm, I wonder?' mumbled Rookwort, thinking out loud.

'Excuse me, but what are you wondering about?' asked Barney politely.

'Eh… What?' Rookwort replied, suddenly focussing on the children once more. 'Oh nothing, I was just thinking out loud.'

But Rookwort was now gazing intently at Katie with a strange expression on his face.

He then asked Katie how Ezekiel was keeping and what he was doing with himself these days. Katie explained about the shop, Mrs Tubbs and how the three guardians had looked after the creatures of Badger Wood without a problem, until now.

'So Ezekiel's still got the Myrtle Cat, eh. She always was special that one,' Rookwort grinned. 'So you know that Myrtle Cats are one of the rarest and wisest creatures in creation. They can live for many, many years, about three or four times our life span. They are also very psychic and can communicate with people telepathically, and possess magical powers, but Tubbsie – well, she was always quite special.'

'Mister Crumpshaw,' Lorna asked suddenly, 'what can you tell us about these Bogwight creatures, I mean are they *really* dangerous?'

'Dangerous indeed, young lady,' replied Rookwort, with a twinkle in his eye. 'No-one with any sense ever messes around with Bogwights, except *me* of course, and believe me, that was very costly! Oh and while you're all here you may as well call me Rook, this *mister* business is making me feel quite old!'

Lenny was about to voice one of his comical quips, but wisely kept his mouth shut as Rookwort gave him a stony stare. It was as though he had been reading Lenny's thoughts, and a good thing too, as Lenny was just about to say that he really was quite old!

'Rook, how can we find out where the Bogwights are?' asked Barney.

Rookwort's head spun round as he snapped, 'Now just hang on a moment! I don't want you children going anywhere near those Bogwights; they're not the friendliest of beings that you could wish to meet. Evil is a better word for them. They don't like anyone or any living creature that is not like them, and believe me, I ought to know.'

'What *exactly*, are they?' asked Lenny.

'H'mm – what indeed,' Rookwort replied thoughtfully. 'Well now, you could say that they don't have any bodies like we do, but they *exist* rightly enough. They're more like half wraiths, you know – half ghost and half flesh really. But they can do living creatures untold damage if they set their evil minds to such a purpose.'

Rookwort paused, letting the gravity of his words settle in the children's thoughts and then added, 'Many years ago, I tried to help one of them and ended up destroying a few Bogwights in the process. But all that they were really after was what little magic that I possessed.'

'Yes,' said Katie. 'Flitter Trott told us that they covet magic.'

'Ah, but not just *any* kind of magic,' replied Rookwort, with a shake of his head, 'because they have no full body of which to speak, Bogwights can't learn magic or cast spells as a human being would. Bogwights have to absorb the *essence* of magic, either by sacrificing the owner of that particular magic and capturing its essence, or by obtaining powerful magical objects which contain some form of magical residue, such as a wand, an amulet or a charm for example.'

Rookwort paused for moment then added, 'That is why I think that they have taken the Foundling. In fact I am certain of it.' He gazed at them all and continued, 'You see, Foundlings are wonderfully magical creatures. Oh yes, we have them in Pangloria too,' he added as he caught the look of surprise reflected in their faces. 'Foundlings can't cast spells or enchantments, but they do carry magical protection by their very existence, and as a result they protect whatever creatures or beings that they live amongst.

'For example in your world, each haven is protected secretly, but here in Pangloria we are more enlightened in the ways of magic and therefore Foundlings offer a different sort of protection, and as such, are guarded more openly. That is why the Bogwights have taken the Foundling of Badger Wood, and my guess is that they will sacrifice her fairly soon.'

'Uncle Rook, Flitter Trott said that if the Bogwights obtain any magic they would use it to harm others, could they really do that?' Katie asked.

'They most certainly could, Katie, and believe me – they will!' replied Rookwort seriously. 'The Bogwights would then subvert the magic and try to find ways to make it grow, and then use it to enforce their dark rule on all living things within Pangloria. They tried once many, many years ago and failed, fortunately, but believe me they will try it again if they get an opportunity!'

He stopped as though brooding on dark thoughts for a few long moments, then his eyes suddenly gleamed with a hint of triumph before he continued. 'Of course, it's only a matter of time before they find a way to open up another portal into your world, and if that happens, who knows what horrors they would inflict on its inhabitants.'

Rookwort stroked his chin, mumbling to himself again for a few moments and then spoke once more to the children as though a plan of action had suddenly come to him. 'Look! I want you all to do something for me, and then I think that I just *may* be able to help you.'

The children all nodded in agreement as Lenny said,

'Sure, Rook, we're game – we'll help you in any way that we can.'

'Good,' replied Rookwort now thoroughly enjoying himself at the prospect of an adventure. 'Barney, I am going to need the use of your bed-scapator, you'll be flying it of course, and I'll need you to come along as well, Katie.'

'But what about us?' cried the twins. 'We don't want to be left behind!'

'Whoa! Now hold on a moment and let me finish what I have to say,' replied Rookwort quickly. 'I need to get to a sea port called Pyton Cove, and pretty quickly, that's why I need Barney and Katie. It just so happens that I know someone there who may be able to give me the information that I need, to help us to rescue the Foundling more quickly.'

The twins were about to voice their protests again, but Rookwort put up a restraining hand. 'What I *need*,' he continued, pointing at the twins, 'is for Bouncer and you two to hold the fort here for me, while we're away. It shouldn't take us more than a few hours.'

'But Rook, why can't we come with you?' asked Lenny.

'*Because*, my eager young jackanapes, the Bogwights may have sensed the use of the magic that you all activated earlier when you roused my mud-beast and decide to come and investigate!

'Now Bogwights don't normally come in this valley you understand, because if there's one thing that they're afraid of its fire, which somehow seems to keep them at bay, and as a matter of fact they're also afraid of one species of living beings, wolves! And Bouncer, I have to say, is as close to a wolf as any dog that *I've* ever seen. But it could be that the Bogwights sense of curiosity, particularly about Barney and his bed-scaptor may overrule their fear and cause them to come poking around, and if they do, I need to know.'

The twins both shrugged and nodded in agreement. 'We could be in for some action then,' replied Lenny in an excited voice.

'Yes you could indeed, my bold young friend,' chuckled Rookwort. 'But do bear in mind that Bogwights are very dangerous creatures and are not to be underestimated, do you understand?'

'Yes,' replied the twins. 'We won't do anything rash; will we, Lenny?' Lorna added, giving her brother a sharp nudge in his ribs with her elbow.

'Humph! Good,' replied Rookwort, narrowing his eyes. 'In that case, you won't mind if I leave some Fire Imps to patrol both ends of the valley.' He smiled to himself as he saw the look of horror on the faces of the twins. 'They won't do you any harm of course, but Fire Imps will keep any unwanted visitors at bay.'

Before anyone could reply, Rookwort said, 'Good, that's sorted then. Best if we start out now, then we can be back before dawn.'

Rookwort stepped out of the cabin, into the dim light of the valley with the children in tow. He walked over to a ring of large, lava-like stones, which completely encircled the old cabin and shouted, 'Stand back! Do not move, or say anything, is that understood!'

The children all nodded and Lorna grasped Bouncer's shaggy mane, keeping him close to her.

Rookwort stood with his thin arms outstretched and his head bent submissively for a while, in total silence. Then concentrating his magic to the peak of its power, he shouted, 'Imparo-Flamaro!' as bolts of silver-coloured lightening lanced from his fingertips, to land at various points on the ground beyond the stone encirclement. As each lightning bolt landed, it left a man sized flame which burned with a bright candle-like glow.

Within each flame a beautiful female imp-like figure danced manically and cackled with glee. Rookwort shouted to them in a commanding voice, 'Welcome, my fiery friends, I have summoned you here for the task of guarding my valley.'

The Fire Imps twittered and cackled with laughter. Rookwort gave them a wry smile and added, 'I also command you this night, to protect these children and their dog from any unwanted visitors.'

The Fire Imps laughed mischievously, with a high pitched twitter. 'Oh Rookwort the magnificent,' they teased, 'so the Bogwights may have caught up with you at last. Even though you are the poorest of wizards, the fact that you have managed to conjure us up at all means that we must obey you.'

Rookwort allowed himself another wry smile at their jest and they added with a shriek of laughter, 'Be assured, wizard, that no Bogwight will get past us to harm the young ones or steal anything that you hold dear. But be careful that when you find the Seer Amarelda, you may learn more that you wished to hear.'

Rookwort chuckled to himself, as he remembered that Fire Imps always spoke in riddles, but were useful beings to have as allies, and besides, this had been one of his more reliable conjurations.

'Hah! Away with your jibes, you impish puppies,' he answered with a laugh. 'Just be sure that you do my bidding.'

In answer the Fire Imps flew high into the air in

different directions across the valley, and with shrieks of mocking laughter, answered, 'Oh yes we will, oh mighty Rookwort.'

Barney looked on in amazement and asked, 'Rook, who is the Seer Amarelda?'

Giving Barney a sideways glance Rookwort replied, 'Oh, she is just someone who may be able to tell me where we may find the Foundling.' Then catching the narrow eyed look that Lorna gave him he added quickly, 'And there could be some other useful information that she may be able to give me.'

Barney nodded dumbly as he stood puzzling upon Rookwort's answer. Rookwort turned to the children and said, 'Well then, my young friends, I suppose that we ought to be moving, the sooner we know what we're facing the better.' He then turned to the twins and added, 'I wouldn't go beyond the encirclement of stones, if I were you. Try to keep within its boundary and make sure that Bouncer does too. There is enough food in there for a month or more, so you won't go hungry, and we should be back within a few hours with any luck.'

'What about those Fire Imp things?' asked Lenny. 'Will they leave us alone?'

'Yes, you should be fine,' replied Rookwort. 'They won't bother you at all, unless *you* bother them of course. Just keep within the stone encirclement and you will be quite safe.'

Rookwort started to walk away and turned back suddenly and said, 'Oh! And one other thing, do not go messing about with any of my instruments under any circumstances, they can be pretty lethal unless you know exactly how to use them.'

Lenny nodded his head, feeling a little disappointed

and asked, 'What are they used for?'

With a knowing expression Rookwort replied, 'Oh, just scientific stuff,' and after giving Lenny a sly smile he turned and walked away with Katie and Barney in tow.

The twins simply looked at each other and raised their eyebrows. Somehow they didn't quite believe him.

As Rookwort, Barney and Katie disappeared out of sight, the twins heard Rookwort shout back at them, 'And don't forget to keep the fire going!'

Barney was the first to spot the bedstead and ran up to it to make sure that it was still intact. Rookwort laughed and said, 'You don't have to worry about your bed-scaptor, not when you're in my valley, and particularly while I am here.'

He walked around the oak bedstead, and with a large grin of admiration said, 'Well, well, so Ezekiel finally let it go, eh?'

Then with a gentle shake of his head Rookwort climbed onto the bedstead and made himself comfortable. 'You're a very lucky young man, Barney, to have a scapator of your very own and at your age too,' Rookwort remarked. 'There are not many of them about now, you know, although I did see one once that was in the form of a toilet of all things! Goodness knows why. It couldn't have been very comfortable!'
Barney and Katie laughed at the thought, and then Barney asked, 'Where are we heading to, Rook?'

Rookwort thought for a moment, and replied, 'Just take us up for now.'

Barney steadied himself and said loudly, 'Bed! Please take us up.' The bedstead lifted itself slowly off the ground then shot high into the air like an elevator.

Once it had reached about three hundred feet above the valley, Rookwort shouted, 'Right! That should do us I think.'

Barney cried out for the bedstead to stop and it halted immediately, and hovered in mid-air. They gazed all around them and Rookwort said to Barney, 'Head for that area of mist over there, but as we get nearer approach it slowly.'

Barney nodded and began to guide the bedstead carefully towards the brooding mist.

'Is that the Rotten Marshes?' Katie asked nervously.

'Yes,' replied Rookwort. 'I just want to check out the ruins, but if I tell you to get us out fast, Barney, you get us out of there like lightning, do you understand?'

Yes, Rook,' replied Barney.

The bedstead sped along as it made its way through the Stag Mountains, sweeping cleanly through its various valleys, sometimes rising and dropping as Barney steered a course towards the dense mist which now began to loom ever closer. As they approached the edges of the mist, Rookwort ordered Barney to slow the bedstead down to a crawl.

Rookwort, who by this time was thoroughly enjoying himself, took what appeared to be a tiny grey iron arrow that was attached to a leather thong from around his neck.

He lifted it up and holding the thong before him said quietly, 'Show me the way to the ruins.' The iron arrow immediately spun a quarter of a turn to their right and remained motionless. Rookwort gave a grunt of satisfaction and said, 'Well, I guess that's where they are, or somewhere about there at any rate. Just follow the Pointer's direction, Barney, but nice and slowly.'

Barney followed Rookwort's instruction, and then

looking over his shoulder asked, 'What *is* that thing Rook?'

'This, my young friend, is a Pointer,' he replied. 'I suppose you could say that it's like a compass, but with a difference. For example, if I'm in a dark place or in a dense mist, I can just ask it to point me in the direction of where I want to go and it will guide me there. It never fails.'

Barney looked at the Pointer once more and thought that it looked strangely similar to the tiny pendant that he had often seen Miss Holfirth wearing.

Yard by yard, the bedstead followed the direction of the Pointer until they found themselves above a pile of huge, stone slabs that looked like the remains of some gigantic structure. They could clearly see a large cave-like entrance at one end of the ruins but saw nothing moving – not even a mouse!

'Okay, Barney,' ordered Rookwort quietly, 'I've seen enough. The Bogwights could be lurking in there, but I need to be absolutely sure. Take us up higher.'

Almost immediately the bedstead had risen quickly upwards, above the dense mist, and they hovered motionless for a time while Rookwort continued to look around.

'Uncle Rook, what was that place down there?' asked Katie.

Rookwort cocked his head to one side, as if he was studying Katie, and with a smile replied, '*That* is where our dreaded enemy may be lurking, Katie, or least I think so. The ruins are the remnants of an ancient stronghold called Krakkenhelm Castle.

'An ancient evil once lurked there many centuries ago until its power was destroyed by a race of powerful white witches and wizards. After that, it fell into the ruins that you now see, but it's my guess that its evil past has attracted the Bogwights, and who knows what else lies in there now. I'll tell you the story of how it was destroyed another time.'

Rookwort took the Pointer from around his neck once more and holding it out in front of him said, 'Show me the way to Pyton Cove.' The Pointer revolved slowly and came to a stop, pointing the way to their destination. 'Okay, Barney, let's get going,' and Rookwort patted the boy on his shoulder. Barney gave the bedstead the command and it took off at top speed, heading towards the mysterious sea port called Pyton Cove.

After they had been flying steadily for just over two hours, Rookwort looked at Katie and Barney and said, 'Now then, the both of you, when we get to Pyton Cove, I want you to stick to me like glue. Say *nothing* to anyone, unless I tell you to. Just let me do the talking. Do you understand?'

Both Barney and Katie nodded. 'Is Pyton Cove dangerous, Uncle Rook?' asked Katie.

'Well, yes it can be,' replied Rookwort. 'You get all sorts of outlandish folk who visit the port from time to time. I often go there to get some of my supplies from the owner of Blaggard's Trading Post, who just happens to be an old and trusted friend of mine. He's a bit of a gruff old sea-dog, but he's as solid as a rock, is old Woodthrop Wyatt. It's him that I'm relying on to arrange for me to talk to the Seer.'

Rookwort reached down into one of the many deep pockets of his tunic and brought out a dark brown leather flask. He pulled the stopper from its neck and took a long drink of the liquid contained in the flask. 'Ah, that's better,' he said with a smile, and then ordered Katie and Barney to drink.

They both looked dubiously at the flask, but Rookwort scolded them and said, 'Come on now! What's the matter with you both? This is my special homemade Spring Mead – it will keep you warm, and keep your strength up. So come on now, drink it; it's good for you!'

Barney took a mouthful of the Spring Mead and felt a glow that seemed to spread right down to his toes and left his stomach feeling strangely full. 'Hey! I like the taste of that, Rook. It really makes you feel warm and cosy inside.'

'I told you so, didn't I?' replied Rookwort with a grin.

Katie coughed and spluttered as she took a sip of the brew, and with both eyes watering, nodded in agreement.

They flew over the Wormwood Wastes for what seemed like hours until they could just make out the silhouette of a distant town on the horizon, and beyond that a large expanse of water which Barney and Katie recognised from the map as the Goranan Sea.

'Now, they get all sorts of seafarers and smugglers in Pyton Cove, and they can be as dangerous as a nest of hornets when they are stirred up. So don't go upsetting any of them or say *anything*. Just remember what I've told you, stick to me like glue,' Rookwort warned, giving both Barney and Katie a hard stare.

They landed the bedstead a few hundred yards from the small town, carefully hiding it in a clump of bushes. Rookwort thrust his hands deep into the pockets of his tunic and pulled out two brown hooded cloaks and a small bag. 'Here, put these on,' he muttered, 'and keep them tight about you, then you won't look out of place.'

Then, opening the small bag, he dipped his hand into it and took a handful of greenish-looking powder which he sprinkled onto the clump of bushes surrounding the bed-scapator. This, Rookwort explained, would conceal the bedstead from any prying eyes.

While he was sprinkling the strange looking powder, Barney and Katie became aware of a revolting smell coming from the bushes, as they both wrinkled their noses in disgust.

'Well! That appears to be working,' said Rookwort with a nod of satisfaction. 'Powdered Grangel Root, it's quite strong isn't it!' he added with a chuckle.

After they had both recovered from a fit of coughing and spluttering at the stench of the Powdered Grangel Root, Katie asked, 'Uncle Rook, you seem to have everything in your pockets, how on earth can your tunic hold so much stuff?'

'That's because it's magic, Katie. Ezekiel gave it to me when he left Pangloria, I honestly don't know how I would have managed without it,' he replied with a smile. 'Why, I can even travel anywhere in Pangloria to get my supplies and carry them back home with almost no effort. It has a number of ever expanding pockets you see, which enables me to carry an extraordinary amount of items, providing that they aren't too large of course.'

Barney and Katie pulled the brown cloaks closely around their shoulders and after Rookwort gave them a grunt of satisfaction they started to walk down into Pyton Cove.

As they all entered the port, Barney and Katie noticed that some of the buildings appeared to be run-down and in a sad state of repair.

They passed a scruffy looking inn that bore the strange name The Bearded Mermaid Tavern. The sign outside of the inn featured an unsavoury picture of a tubby looking mermaid who had a burly face and a large bushy beard. A couple of surly, rough looking men, wearing ragged seafaring clothes, eyed them up slyly as they quickly walked past the tavern.

Barney and Katie glanced nervously at each other and were now almost running in an attempt to keep pace with Rookwort. They continued to walk past various rundown cottages and huts until at last they came upon a small quay where the saw a couple of tall-masted ships lying at anchor in the tiny cove.

At the far end of the quayside they saw a large wooden cabin with a sign above its door which read Blaggard's Trading Post, proprietor Woodthrop Wyatt.

Sitting in a rocking chair upon the timber porch at the front of the building sat a large, scruffy looking man who was puffing contentedly on a small clay pipe. He was busy whittling a piece of wood with a razor-sharp knife and skilfully forming a small three-masted sailing ship. As the three of them stepped up on to the porch the old man looked up and his grizzled face broke into a grin as he spoke in a gruff voice.

'Well, well, well. If it isn't me old matey Rookwort Crumpshaw, and what will you be wanting? Supplies? But no, it'll be something else I'm thinking,' he continued as he narrowed his eyes shrewdly.

'Well met, Woody, my old friend,' replied Rookwort, giving Barney and Katie a sly wink. 'I'm afraid that I'm in a bit of a fix and in need of your help again.'

'Nothing new there then!' snorted Woodthrop with a laugh. 'What is it this time, Rook?'

'Bogwights,' replied Rookwort evenly.

'Bogwights!' growled Woodthrop, raising an enormous pair of bushy eyebrows. 'Why do you want to go messing about with them again?' He paused for a moment and giving Rookwort a look of exasperation said, 'Listen, you great bumbling excuse for a wizard, I like to think that as we've been doing business since I don't know when, that we are friends of a sort. So I'll be giving you some good advice. You've always had more sand than brains, matey, but this time, you just leave those stinking Bogwights alone; then maybe, just maybe, you'll live a little longer. Do you catch my drift, matey? Or does that stubborn, landlubber's head of yours refuse to see sense?'

Rookwort roared with laughter, and with a shrug of his shoulders, he replied, 'I can't this time, old friend.' He jerked his thumb backwards as he added, 'For their sakes. Ezekiel has sent them to rescue a creature that the Bogwights have taken. So I need your help to speak to the Seer.'

'What, Old Amarelda? How's she going to help,' grunted Woodthrop in surprise, 'and who are these youngsters?'

Rookwort beckoned Barney and Katie forward and told them to lower their hoods. 'This here is young Barney and my niece Katie,'

'Oh, niece is it,' replied Woodthrop letting out a whistle of surprise. 'Well isn't that something.' He gave them both a smile and added, 'I'm the owner of this here establishment, my name's Woodthrop Wyatt, ex-captain of the *Oranor Star*, at your service, but any friend of Rook's can call me Woody.'

'Well, Woody, what do you say? Can you fix it so as we can have a chat with the Seer or not?' Rookwort asked.

Woody stared at Rookwort, his bushy eyebrows bristling over his sharp searching eyes, and replied, 'Oh alright, I'll see what I can do, but you'll have to look after the store while I'm gone mind.'

Rookwort nodded and Woody got up out of his chair, pulled on an oilskin cape and said, 'And don't go eating me out of house and home while I'm gone!' Then stepping through the door, he made his way up the cobbled street towards The Bearded Mermaid Tavern.

Katie and Barney gazed around the store and saw an array of sacks containing grain, beans and a selection of strange looking fruit and vegetables. They also found a large number of stone jars with wooden stoppers in them, all containing different liquids. On one side of the store they saw shelf after shelf of linen and furs, also huge baskets which were filled with a variety of dried fish and bread. Giant legs of smoked ham and mutton hung from the rafters of the store. Under a large canvas sail they found dozens of barrels, which Rookwort quickly covered back up.

'Smuggled brandy I guess,' admitted Rookwort with a grin. 'Good old Woody; he never was one to refuse a bit of contraband.'

Katie turned to her uncle and asked, 'Who *is* Woody?'

Rookwort thought for a moment and replied, 'He is what you see, Katie. If you want anything, or you need any information in these parts, then Woody's your man. There's a lot goes on in that grizzled old head of his and if I ever need any information about what's happening to the folk of Pangloria you can bet that Woody knows. Mind you, he has to deal with some unsavoury characters, including me,' Rookwort added, giving Katie a sly wink.

Before long Woody returned. 'Well, it's all fixed up,' he said gruffly as he entered the store. 'She'll see you now, but you'll have to be paying her, Rook; times are very lean for her and she has to keep body and soul together somehow.'

'How much?' asked Rookwort.

'Fifty silver pieces should do it,' Woody replied evenly. 'My time is free, but you owe me one, Rook!'

Rookwort reached into his tunic and pulled out four flasks of Spring Mead and smiled. 'I'm sure that these will come in handy, Woody, they'll help to keep out the chill from those salty bones of yours.'

'Har, har, matey, I see that you've still got that old tunic of Ezekiel's,' Woody replied with a wheezy laugh. 'What would I give for that. I wouldn't need the store then, and I could just pop all of my goods in that tunic and be away, selling it all around Pangloria. Ah well,' Woody gave a wistful sigh, 'you lot had better be away and see Amarelda, she's waiting for you.'

Rookwort purchased a few supplies and put them into several pockets of his tunic, then after shaking Woody warmly by the hand, stepped out into the cobbled street. With Barney and Katie in tow, he set off towards the Seer's cottage, following the directions that Woody had given them.

~ CHAPTER NINE ~

Rookwort Plans a Rescue

After walking past The Bearded Mermaid Tavern they came upon a tiny but quaint-looking grey stone cottage which had a roof that was the hull of old upturned boat. Poking out of the roof was a crooked metal chimney which puffed out a steady stream of smoke.

Rookwort walked up to the front of the cottage and knocked gently on the door. They heard a croaky voice inviting them inside. 'Come on in, the door isn't locked!'

Rookwort opened the door and the three of them stepped inside into a pokey little parlour. Sitting next to a small black stove was a wizened old woman with an enormous mane of shaggy grey hair.

The Seer Amarelda was neatly dressed in a vivid green top and a crimson skirt, topped off with a bright yellow woollen shawl. She was straining to see them in the dim light, through a pair of round spectacles which housed a pair of thick glass lenses.

As they drew closer to the old woman, Barney noted that her eyes were a vivid green colour and she seemed to see right through them all.

'Ah, what is this that I see?' she croaked as her aged hands reached out towards Katie. 'One of a witch's brood, eh? Come closer, my child,' she cooed, beckoning Katie to come closer.

The old woman clasped Katie's hand gently between her own and added, 'Oh yes, definitely one of a witch's brood. I sense very great magic in this one. A *powerful* white witch I would say, or I'm no seer at all.'

Before the Seer could utter another word Rookwort rounded on Katie and Barney and snapped, 'You two! Out! Now! Go on, wait outside!'

'But Uncle Rook,' Katie stammered.

'Do as you are told, girl! Get outside now!'

Both Barney and Katie did as Rookwort ordered and as they turned and stepped back out through the cottage door, they heard a cackle of laughter, as the old woman taunted them, 'Come back and see me again soon, my dear.'

Barney could see that Katie was shocked by the encounter and saw that tears had begun to well up in her eyes. He stepped up to her and said quietly, 'Are you okay Katie?'

'Yes – I think so,' she mumbled, trying hard to hold back her tears. 'I wonder what she meant by one of a witch's brood?'

Barney shrugged his shoulders and shook his head, 'I don't know,' he sighed. 'Maybe Rook will tell us later,' he added, but somehow he didn't think that Rookwort would.

They both placed their ears against the door of the cottage as they heard Rookwort's muffled voice ask the Seer, 'What do you *mean* she's descended from a white witch?'

The talking suddenly grew quieter; all that Barney and Katie could now hear were low murmuring voices as Amarelda and Rookwort continued to speak in hushed tones.

In the end both Barney and Katie gave up trying to make any sense of the whispered conversation coming from within the cottage, and moved away from the door to sit down on the low wall.

Barney gazed at Katie, who still appeared to be upset and asked, 'Do you get a feeling that something isn't right here? You know – like there's something that that Rook hasn't told us?'

'Yes,' she replied quietly, 'I was just thinking the same thing myself. There are quite a few questions that I would like Uncle Rook and Uncle Ezekiel to answer.'

After what seemed like an age, the door of the cottage opened and out stepped Rookwort with a disturbed look on his craggy face. 'Okay you two! Let's get going, it's getting dark and we need to be on our way.'

'What about the things that the Seer said?' Katie asked, grasping her uncle's arm.

He shrugged her arm away and quickly headed back up the cobbled street and out of Pyton Cove. 'There isn't any time to speak of this now, girl. I will tell you later; now come on, we *must* hurry,' he ordered once more, as he began to walk at quite a fast pace.

They reached the clump of bushes where they had concealed the bed-scapator and quickly climbed aboard.

Rookwort turned to Barney and snapped, 'Just tell the bed-scapator to take us back to the Valley of the Fiery Holes! It should know the way by now!'

By this time it was beginning to grow darker as the dusk crept upon them, so Barney shouted the instructions to the bedstead, which responded smoothly and sped off, back towards Rookwort's home.

Meanwhile, many miles away, back in Rookwort's cabin, darkness had already fallen and both of the twins were dozing on top of Rookwort's bed. They were roused suddenly by a low growl of warning from Bouncer. 'What is it, boy?' whispered Lenny urgently, seeing that the hackles on Bouncer's neck had risen and that he had stepped protectively towards the door.

'I think that he's heard something and wants to go outside,' Lorna replied. So slowly and very quietly, they eased the cabin door open and stepped out into the night!

As the bedstead flew back to the Valley of the Fiery Holes, Rookwort had been giving Katie a series of sidelong glances before he finally asked, 'This shop of Ezekiel's – tell me about it.'

Katie told him everything that she knew, how long her uncle Ezekiel had been in the shop and what sort of items he sold.

Rookwort nodded his head and asked, 'Tell me about your mother Pandora. What did she look like? What type of person was she?'

Katie described her mother and how she had been particularly attached to Ezekiel. There were tears in her eyes as she told him how Pandora had died when Katie was quite young, and how she had been left to be brought up mainly by her father and Ezekiel.

They fell silent for a while before Rookwort asked quietly, 'Katie, does Ezekiel ever have any other visitors to his shop other than customers? You know – *regular* visitors.'

Katie paused to think for a moment and replied, 'Well, he gets people coming in all of the time, to browse around and buy stuff if you know what I mean, but no one visits regularly – unless you count Barney's school teacher,' she paused for a moment and exclaimed, 'Oh drat, I've forgotten her name.'

'Miss Holfirth,' answered Barney. 'Her first name is Agnes – well that's what my mum calls her.'

'What does she look like?' Rookwort demanded.

As Barney described her, he noticed that a strange gleam had crept into Rookwort's eyes as he turned to ask Katie another question. 'Has this Agnes Holfirth ever visited the shop while you were staying with Ezekiel?'

'Yes Uncle,' replied Katie. 'Do you know, I've never thought about it before, but she always seems to pop into the shop when I'm there and buys a little something or other, and fusses over me a little; she's really ever such a kind lady.'

'Not if you're in her class she isn't,' Barney quipped.

'Ah,' mumbled Rookwort under his breath. 'That explains a lot.'

'Explains what?' enquired Katie.

'Oh nothing that I'm sure about yet,' replied Rookwort rather too quickly, I'll explain it to you some other time.'

Katie was about to say that her uncle could explain it all now, but she noticed that he appeared to have become moody and irritable again, so decided to let the matter rest at least for the time being.

As the twins and Bouncer became accustomed to the darkness about them, they saw dark shadows moving about beyond the stone encirclement. As each shadow attempted to move closer, the bright candle-like flame of a Fire Imp would appear directly in front of it, growing larger and brighter, as it drove each shadowy figure away, giggling with their high pitched laughter as they did so. After this had happened a number of times the twins heard the shadows hiss in frustration, as they began to slowly retreat back out of the valley.

The Fire Imps had done their work well, and as they both still felt a little tired, the twins and Bouncer went back inside Rookwort's cabin and once more fell into a gentle sleep.

As the bedstead flew towards the Valley of the Fiery Holes, Barney began to think about how they were going to actually rescue the Foundling, and how they would carry it. He knew from what Flitter Trott had told them that it had to be fairly quickly.

Both Katie and Rookwort had become very quiet and appeared to be deep in thought, so Barney wisely decided not to ask any further questions, and commanded the bedstead to fly faster.

The bedstead immediately responded and flew like the wind back towards the Valley of the Fiery Holes.

Barney brought the bedstead round in a wide circle, and landed it smoothly just inside of the stone encirclement, and the three of them climbed down off the bed and headed towards the cabin.

The door opened quickly as Bouncer and the twins came bounding towards them. 'We knew that you were back!' cried Lorna excitedly. 'Bouncer woke us up to tell us.' Bouncer ran around them all, barking excitedly as Rookwort smiled and asked, 'Well, you two, have you anything to report?'

'Just a minor skirmish, but the Fire Imps saw them off without any bother,' replied Lenny with a smug grin. 'How did you three get on?' he asked eager for news of their journey.

'Let's get inside and I'll explain,' replied Rookwort.

'Oh that *will* make a change!' exclaimed Katie sarcastically, as she scowled at her uncle.

Rookwort pretended that he hadn't heard Katie's remark, as he thought to himself, don't bite and don't be drawn. Remain focussed on what is really important for now. You can explain about the Seer another time.

They all tumbled into the cabin and were soon seated around the table enjoying a well-earned meal of smoked ham and eggs, washed down with mugs of honeyed herb tea, while Bouncer lay close to the fire gnawing noisily on a large marrow bone.

After they had eaten, Rookwort drew their attention and demanded silence, as he started to pace up and down the length of the cabin.

'I want to begin by explaining to you all about Pangloria's three moons.' Catching the puzzled looks on their faces, he added, 'Oh don't look so surprised! Many worlds have more than one moon, just look at the planets within your own solar system, some have none at all and some have many moons.'

He paused for a moment then continued with his explanation, 'Pangloria is really no different to your world, except that its moons have a greater effect up on it when they *all* appear in the evening sky together, and particularly when they are all in-line with each other.'

'Do Pangloria's moons all have names?' Lorna asked eagerly.

Rookwort gazed at her, thinking to himself how the inquisitive nature of children never failed to amaze him. Feeling like a school teacher giving a lesson in astronomy, he replied, 'In Pangloria, its three moons are known as Gatalei – the green, which is the largest of the three moons. Oranor – the blue, which the second largest. The smallest of the three is Remar – the red. Whenever the three moons are in perfect alignment it is known here on Pangloria as a Three Moon Equinox, and its effect on anything magical is very potent.'

'I suppose that's why the Bogwights took the Foundling at this time,' Lorna, commented.

'It most certainly is,' replied Rookwort. 'They couldn't steal a Foundling within Pangloria especially at this time, because the Three Moon Equinox only occurs once every thousand years. Therefore, its effect will strengthen the magic within each Foundling enormously. As a result, any Foundling within Pangloria will be protected more closely by their guardians. Remember, the guardians have sworn to protect them *even* if it should cost them their lives.'

Rookwort looked at each of the children in turn, as it was vital that they clearly understood all that he had told them and that they were giving him their full attention before he continued. 'My guess is that the Bogwights knew this and very cleverly set me up, in order to open up a portal into your world. This of course enabled them to cross over and steal the Foundling of Badger Wood.'

Barney looked up at Rookwort and asked, 'But how would the Bogwights know about the existence of our world and Badger Wood or its Foundling?'

Rookwort stroked his chin thoughtfully and considered Barney's shrewd question before he answered. 'Many hundreds of years ago Pangloria was in great danger of being conquered by a most evil wizard called the Ice King. He had just one aim and that was to cover the whole of Pangloria in a veil of cold and ice and to rule over all of its peoples. His most loyal servants were Bogwights, and as a reward they would have had every person and creature of Pangloria to prey upon and enslave.

'They were given a few bits of minor magic of course, just to keep them loyal to the Ice King, along with a stronghold in the Rotten Marshes. The Ice King was finally vanquished however, mainly due to an alliance of wizards and witches, along with some of the peoples of Pangloria, and so final was his defeat that he was destined never ever to return to the living world.

'His servants, the Bogwights, simply disappeared out of sight for a time, but they are still here in Pangloria, only far fewer in numbers. The small amount of magic that they possess must have been enough for them to have discovered the existence of your world and its havens, and of course the Foundling of Badger Wood.

'All that they needed to know was how to gain access to the portal between your world and Pangloria, which they tricked me into opening of course!'

The children had listened in awe to Rookwort's tale and were still trying to comprehend everything that he had told them when Lenny asked, 'Just when is this Equinox supposed to take place?'

'Tonight,' Rookwort replied dropping his bombshell and smiling grimly as he saw the shock register on their faces. 'You see, the Bogwights have been very clever; they knew all about your world and that it too had a number of Foundlings. They probably gambled on the fact that the Foundlings weren't as closely guarded in your world as they are here on Pangloria. That's mainly due to the fact that not everyone in your world believes that magic really exists. Wouldn't *you* take a gamble on such a thing?'

'When can we set out and see this thing through?' asked Lenny eagerly.

'As soon as we've rested and made our preparations, my bold young friend,' replied Rookwort with a roar of laughter, 'and not a moment before.'

Rookwort decided that for the remainder of that day, Katie, Barney and he would catch up on some needed rest while the twins and Bouncer kept guard.

After a few hours' sleep they were duly woken by the twins for a meal of bread and cheese, washed down with some of Rookwort's reviving Spring Mead. This left them all feeling totally refreshed, even Bouncer lapped up the brew that Rookwort had poured into a small clay bowl and was wagging his tail excitedly.

'Right,' said Rookwort. 'This is how I think that we should go about our business tonight.'

The children listened very carefully as Rookwort explained how he and Katie would go on ahead of Barney and the twins, as a small vanguard.

The children immediately began to protest, but Rookwort held up his hand and said, 'No! It *has* to be this way, or not at all! I don't want you to worry about Katie or myself. I have enough magic in me to protect us both, even if I do get it wrong at times!'

Katie looked at her uncle with a worried expression on her face, as he explained, 'I intend to flush the Bogwights out into the centre of their lair. We just don't have the time to find out where they are keeping the Foundling locked away, so we will need to time our rescue precisely, just as they are about to carry out their foul rite!'

Barney frowned as he asked, 'But Rook, won't that be too risky? We may not get to her in time?'

'Yes,' replied Rookwort, 'it *will* be risky – but not as risky as if we don't flush them out. We need all of the Bogwights to be present during the rite of the Three Moon Equinox, that way we can be fairly sure that none of them can jump in and take us by surprise. I only intend to be ahead of you and Bouncer by a few minutes. You see, the Bogwights will be so eager to get their revenge on me because I am their greatest enemy. And you can be certain that they will all come out of their hiding places, in force, just to get their filthy hands on me! Of course, by then you will all have arrived in time to support Katie and safely snatch the Foundling!'

The children all looked at each other dubiously, and Lenny shrugged his shoulders and voiced their doubts, 'This all sounds fine, Rook, but what about Katie? How is she going to defend herself? And how are we going to be of any help?'

Rookwort gave them all another one of his mocking smiles and said, 'Do you really think that I would let you all go into the Bogwights infernal lair without giving you some form of protection? Follow me! All of you!' he commanded, and leading them outside close to the edge of the stone encirclement, he beckoned Katie to come forward, and grasping both of her hands gently in his within own, he said, 'I want you to trust me, girl, and do everything that I ask of you. Do you understand?'

Katie nodded her head slowly.

'Good,' said Rookwort giving her a faint smile. 'I

have a strong feeling that somehow this *is* going to work.'

Before Katie could ask why, Rookwort explained, 'Now I want you to hold out your right arm in front of you and point to that large grey rock – the one with the large white fleck in it.'

Katie raised her eyebrows but did as her uncle had instructed.

Then she heard Rookwort's commanding voice say, 'Concentrate on that rock and *see* only that rock, in your mind. Heed no sound, other than my voice.'

Katie turned to stare at her uncle and stammered, 'But Uncle Rook!'

'I said *concentrate*! Do as I ask and *focus*! Become as one with the rock,' urged Rookwort.

Katie concentrated on the large grey rock, noting every one of its details and flaws. She suddenly saw with great clarity the curve of the white marbled fleck, with its silver veins and the sparkle of the metallic fragments embedded with the stone.

'Good,' whispered her uncle gently. 'Now keep your focus upon the rock and think about something that makes you very angry.'

At first Katie began to falter, but as Rookwort urged her once more she then began searching back through her memories. Katie thought about how angry she had felt on the day that her mother had died and about the sadness of her tragic loss at such a young age. *Why? Why, did it happen to me?*

She could feel the anger building up inside her again. *How could my mother leave me? I was only a small child, how could she? How could she?*

Katie felt so angry that she was only dimly aware of her uncle's voice as it softly cajoled and encouraged her,

'Now Katie, let your anger go. Focus all of it into that rock – get rid of your pent up anger – do it – do it now!'

Barney and the twins watched in awe as Katie began to shake uncontrollably. They saw the grim determination etched on her face as she slowly let the magic build up within her.

Suddenly they gasped, as a golden coloured lightning bolt shot from her fingers, directly into the large grey rock which immediately disappeared in a hissing cloud of dust!

Katie's arm fell heavily to her side as she turned towards them all, her forehead beaded in sweat and her face chalk-white, she stammered, 'Uncle Rook, I – I didn't know that I could do that.'

'No and neither did I, until now that is,' he murmured quietly. 'Although, I have to say, that I *did* suspect it. Look, Katie, I can't say too much right now, but I will try and tell you what I know after we've rescued the Foundling – that's a promise.'

Katie nodded and rather shakily she moved to sit down on a nearby rock.

'Okay, now for you three!' Rookwort urged. 'We're going to need something that you can use as missiles against the Bogwights – a few small rocks or pebbles maybe? We need to arm you with some form of fire-wielding weapon.'

Barney grinned as he and the twins reached into their back pockets and pulled out their catapults and marbles. 'Do you think that these will do?' asked Lenny.

'Let me have a look at those,' said Rookwort with interest, taking both the 'Y' shaped sticks and the marbles. 'What *are* they?'

'Catapults,' replied Lorna, 'and we're the best shots

in Plummington,' she added proudly. 'Lenny can hit the target every time, can't he, Barney?' Barney nodded as Rookwort stooped down to pick up a small stone.

Carefully rolling it in his fingers, he placed it on one of the boulders of the encirclement, and moving back to the children, he said to Lenny, 'Show me!'

Lenny winked at Barney and Lorna, and after loading up his catapult with a fiery coloured marble proceeded to shoot the stone neatly off the boulder.

'Well done, Lenny! That was *some* shot,' Rookwort announced, looking very impressed. As he stooped to pick up the marble that Lenny had just shot, he asked him, 'Do you know what this is?'

'Oh it's just a pretty-looking marble that we got from Old Zeke's shop,' replied Lorna, with a shrug.

'Oh I think you'll find that it's rather more than that,' Rookwort answered knowingly. 'This just happens to be a Fire-Stone. If I put just a little of my magic into it, watch what happens.'

Rookwort asked the children to put all of their marbles into one pile. Then moving towards them, he made several passes over the bright glass orbs with his hands as he began to weave his magic into them.

The marbles began to glow brightly as if they were on fire, and as soon as the glow had vanished, Rookwort handed them the Fire Stones. As Barney and the twins gazed into the depths of their marbles they were astonished to see fiery flames dancing within each glass orb.

Rookwort ordered Lenny to shoot at another small rock, which promptly exploded with an almighty flash as Lenny's Fire-Stone struck it.

'Wow!' yelled Barney. 'That was brilliant! I can't wait to use these on the Bogwights.'

'I bet you can't,' Rookwort chuckled, as he gave Barney a look of warning, 'but you may be well armed but you still need to be very careful, especially with Bogwights. This isn't a game or an innocent bit of target practice that we're undertaking, you know – you all need to remember that.'

They all trooped back into the cabin where Rookwort told them to get a few more hours of sleep. 'You will certainly need it before this night is through, so off to bed with you all and try to get some sleep.'

They all settled down as comfortably as they could and soon fell into an uneasy slumber as they thought about the battle ahead.

Barney was woken by a gentle prod on his shoulder as Rookwort's voice said quietly, 'Come on, young sleepy head, it's time you were awake, we'll all need to get moving fairly soon.'

As Barney sat up he felt the caress of a large wet tongue on his face. 'Aw – gerr-off, Bouncer!' he moaned, as everyone else giggled loudly.

'Right you lot,' said Rookwort seriously. 'We'll need to get moving soon, so I want you to make sure that you've all got the cloaks I gave you earlier. It's no good being in a dangerous place and being cold as well. That would never do.'

Rookwort then went over the rescue plan with them in great detail, asking each of them questions and getting them to repeat everything to make sure that they fully understood what was expected of them. Finally, he gave a grunt of satisfaction and said, 'Okay, have you all got your weapons and your supply of Fire-Stones?' The children nodded and Rookwort took a deep breath and added, 'In that case, we may as well get going.'

He quickly unbarred the door and stepped outside

into the darkness with Bouncer and the children following close behind.

As they were all climbing aboard the bedstead, Barney noted with some surprise that no matter how many people climbed aboard there always seemed to be enough room to accommodate them all.

Rookwort instructed Barney to take the bed-scaptor high up into the air and within moments they had soared to a height of several hundred feet above the valley. As they looked around them Lorna suddenly pointed and exclaimed, 'Oh look at the moons!' They all gazed up into the clear star-clustered sky and saw three moons.

The nearest moon, Oranor, which appeared to be the prettiest of the three, was a pale blue colour. The middle moon, Gatalei, looked very similar to the Earth's moon, but had a greenish tinge, making it look like a large opal hanging in the sky. The third moon, Remar, on the other hand, was a ruby red colour but looked faraway and forbidding.

Rookwort gazed at them for a time in silence, and then said, 'Pretty aren't they? You're all very lucky to see such a sight, particularly on your first visit to Pangloria. But I'm afraid that we don't have much time for star-gazing tonight, we've got a rescue to carry out, and we'd better get moving!'

Using the Pointer, Rookwort gave Barney careful directions and the bedstead took off at a steady pace towards the Rotten Marshes and the Bogwights' lair.

After flying for a while they finally reached the edge of the Rotten Marshes, and Rookwort asked Barney to circle around its edge in order to spy out the lay of the land. They all noticed that the area was still covered in a blanket of dense mist, except at its very centre, where they spotted the ruins of an ancient structure.

'The Bogwights must have found a way to drive the mist back and prevent it from covering the ruins. You see, they have to have a clear line of sight of the equinox as they perform the rite or it will not be a success,' said Rookwort, pointing at the ruins far below.

'Uncle, couldn't you just perform a spell to fill the sky with dense clouds or something in order to mask their view of the equinox?' asked Katie.

'Well, I suppose that I could do that easily enough,' replied Rookwort, 'but it's just too risky. What if for some reason the spell didn't work? And besides, the Bogwights would just slaughter the Foundling anyway. No, we're far safer sticking to our original plan.'

They flew carefully to within several hundred yards from the edge of the ruins, where Rookwort asked Barney to land.

Barney brought the bedstead to a smooth stop and gently lowered it onto the spongy ground. Katie and Rookwort dismounted gingerly, and as they stepped down they felt the boggy ground give a little under their feet.

Rookwort gave Barney and the twins a serious stare for a moment and said, 'Now remember what I told you, give me about two minutes, and then *carefully* make your way through the entrance into the ruins using the bed-scapator, do you understand?' The children nodded.

'Good. If you hear either of us calling, you must come to our aid quickly, shooting those Fire-Stones! And do *try* to avoid hitting Katie or me,' he added grimly. Then as they pulled their cloaks around them tightly, Katie and Rookwort turned and walking away slowly, disappeared into the dense mist.

Barney and the twins waited for what seemed like hours, listening for the slightest sound, but all that they could hear were their own hearts beating loudly and an occasional muffled whimper from Bouncer.

Lenny looked at his watch and said, 'It's been more than two minutes! Come on, let's make a move! Besides, I'm sure that this wretched mist has got even thicker while we've been sitting here.'

'I thought that it had too,' replied Lorna. 'It seems so creepy, like it wants to swallow you up or something. Come on, Barney, let's follow them.'

Barney nodded his head in agreement and began to move the bedstead slowly forward, a yard at a time until they came to a sudden stop, up against a huge piece of the stone ruin.

'What do we do now?' cried Barney in panic. 'I can't even see where we came from or which way we have to go.'

'There's only one thing for it,' replied Lenny with a shrug. 'We'll just have to go up above the mist, find our bearings, and then come straight back down again.'

Carefully Barney took the bedstead up vertically, into the clear sky, but as they stared down towards the ground, they could see nothing at all except for the thick blanket of the mist which clung to its surface. Barney carefully landed the bedstead again and the children began to search around them as the mist grew ever thicker. Even the sound of their voices appeared to be muffled by its unfriendly swirl.

Barney turned to the twins and said glumly, 'Looks like we're going to have to face it, we're lost! But what makes it worse is that Katie and Rook are in those ruins, all on their own and we can't help them!'

~ CHAPTER TEN ~

Fire-Stones versus Bogwights

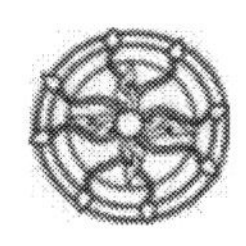

Using the Pointer to guide them, Katie and Rookwort made their way carefully across the boggy ground of the Rotten Marshes. At first they seemed to be making little progress due to the ground being so spongy, but as they got used to the terrain their steps became lighter and quicker, and slowly they drew nearer to the dark, cave-like entrance.

When they finally reached the entrance to the Bogwights lair Rookwort called a momentarily halt to their march. Reaching deep into one of the pockets of his tunic, he pulled out two torches made from a Panglorian bulrush reed, which had been soaked in a rubbery pitch. Preferring not to use magic at this point, he used a large silver headed match which he produced from another of the pockets in his tunic; striking it quickly between his fingers it instantly burst into flame. Carefully he lit both torches, handing one to Katie, and although they didn't burn too brightly, the torches gave off enough light for them to see ahead in the darkness.

'These won't last for too long, so we'll have to move quickly,' said Rookwort quietly, and he started to move again, at a faster pace through the entrance of the Bogwights' lair.

After fifty yards or so they suddenly emerged into a wide, cavernous tunnel. As Katie and Rookwort continued past the entrance for several steps, they appeared to be walking on a hardened clay surface which quickly merged into a wide cobblestone path. Walking deeper into the ruins they descended down a gradual slope which continued on for as far as their eyes could see.

Their eyes soon adjusted to the dimly lit surroundings, and they began to move at a quicker pace through the tunnel. But even though they tried to move carefully and quietly the sound of their footsteps ringing on the cobblestone path reverberated in their ears.

Katie looked about her nervously and with a whisper said, 'Uncle Rook, I hope the Bogwights can't hear us.'

'Oh they'll certainly know that we are here by now,' Rookwort answered with a smile, 'and that is just what I am hoping for. I want them all together when we confront them. That, Katie, will be their undoing!'

Ezekiel Crumpshaw stared at Flitter Trott and the Maiden and with a frown of deep concern etched into his face said, 'There's no need to apologise, Flit. I know that both Sylvania and you didn't want to drag me out on a night like this, but believe me I really am grateful and so very glad that I came.'

As the three guardians examined the trees near to the Goblin Oak they saw that the Black Wilt was now beginning to take hold, and also saw to their horror that some of the trees were already beginning to show signs of rotting. Large sections of bark were already beginning to peel away and spores of a black fungus were starting to eat away the heart of the worst afflicted trees.

'It's not just the trees, Ezekiel,' cried Flitter Trott. 'I've found whole nests of insects, weasels and birds that have just... died! We must be able to do something.'

The Maiden was slowly pacing back and forth, carefully looking around her and assessing the damage that had already been wrought by the Black Wilt. Suddenly she stopped pacing and stared at Ezekiel with a slight narrowing of her bright blue eyes. She appeared to be wrestling with her emotions as she searched for a solution, and then gave a long sigh before she asked, 'Ezekiel, what do you know of magical blood rites?'

'Ma'am, how can you contemplate such a thing?' cried Flitter Trott in alarm. 'Blood rites go against everything that we represent or believe in.'

'I know Flit, *really* I do,' replied the Maiden softly. 'But do you want the wood and every creature in it to decay and die horribly? We have to buy the children some time, and try to delay the pestilence until the Foundling is returned. That's if she is not dead already. What do you think, Ezekiel?'

Ezekiel pursed his lips before answering. 'I don't think that the Bogwights have sacrificed her yet, Sylvania. If they had, I am sure that we would have sensed it somehow. As for a magical blood rite, it might just work, although the shedding of blood does tend to be an earthly pagan ritual, which is often scoffed at and even despised these days. However, I am more than willing to try anything which will buy the children some time and extend the life of the wood, even if it is just for a single day.'

The Maiden grasped Ezekiel's hand gently and asked, 'You are the most practised and wisest of the three of us. Are you willing to utter the words of the blood rite, here and now, within the heart of the wood?' There was a pleading look in her eyes, as Ezekiel saw the tears beginning to well up in them.

Slowly he nodded his head in acceptance. 'I was thinking more in terms of a combination of both healing and sympathetic magic. It would of course involve a gift of blood, but that would be more of a symbolic aspect of the ritual which I have in mind.'

Ezekiel then began to explain about the ritual that he had in mind.

After Ezekiel had finished, Flitter Trott moved towards the Maiden, and placing his tiny hand on her arm said, 'If you and Ezekiel are resolved on this then so am I. As much as I abhor the shedding of blood, I refuse to let these evil wraiths destroy everything that we have worked for and protected for so long.'

'Thank you, Flit,' she replied with a smile, as she fought back her tears.

Together, they climbed the steep slopes of the Mound slowly and steadily until they stood upon its flattened summit. The Maiden began to chant the words of magic, as she laid a sprinkling of salt, carefully forming a circle of protection. At its northern point Ezekiel laid a handful of freshly dug earth, upon which he placed a small branch of alder that had become infected by the Black Wilt.

Meanwhile, Flitter Trott had placed a burning brand of a bulrush at the southern point of the circle, and a small bowl of water at its western point. The Maiden placed a single white dove feather on the circle's eastern point. Together, each of the offerings presented the four elements of Earth, Air, Fire and Water.

When they had completed their preparations, each guardian stood in the centre of the circle of protection, and Ezekiel with his arms held high above his head, began to call upon the cosmic power of the Damsel. After several long minutes of contemplation, they came together and held each other's hands, forming a tiny circle within a circle of protection, and began to slowly move widdershins (whenever wizards and witches move in an anti-clockwise direction within a magical circle it is given the name of Widdershins), almost dancing as they did so as they prepared themselves mentally for the ritual.

They stopped suddenly and moved into the centre of the circle facing towards its outer edge. Ezekiel began to utter the words of the supplication, as they stood with their heads bowed and their arms crossed upon their chests. And in total silence, each of the guardians began to concentrate their healing thoughts and power, focussing them towards the aspect of goodness and the magical oath of protection.

The Maiden then took the small curved Athame from the cord tied around her slender waist and holding it up high in front of her, blessed it, making it ready for the final stage of the rite.

Each guardian in turn held out their left hand, and gave the Maiden a solemn bow as she gently pricked each of their thumbs, including her own. She then caught a single drop of their blood in a tiny crystal phial. The Maiden then turned to Ezekiel and handed him the crystal phial and returned once more to her appointed place within the circle.

Ezekiel moved to the northern point of the circle and carefully poured the drops of precious blood onto the small pile of earth. Raising his arms he uttered the final words of the rite. 'Oh beloved mother of creation and the essence of the cosmos, by this pricking of our thumbs, accept this, the sacred gift of our blood and our pledge. Please give your protection to your children and our sworn charges, this night until the resolution of the coming dawn.'

Almost instantly a faint red mist arose about them and slowly began to spread as it travelled outwards form the depths of Badger Wood.

They raised their bowed heads as the waif-like figure of a woman appeared before them. She was clad in a simple white cloak, her features giving the guardians an impression of ageless beauty.

As always, the Damsel appeared in a veil of silver light, and giving them all a benign smile, she began to speak to each of them within their minds:

'My guardians and beloved children, the gift that you have offered this night is not one that I would normally accept. However, because of the ills that have been wrought on this haven, it is acceptable to me nonetheless. It is a selfless offering that is well given and will indeed stem the decay, at least for a little while. But the protection that you have gained, will only last until the first light of dawn or the first cock-crow of the coming morn.

'I know that the fate of this haven now rests upon

our brother Rookwort, four brave children and the courage of a dog. But be assured that they are committed in this venture and even as we all stand here are entering into the final stage of their quest. Do not despair, have faith in the choices that you have made.'

With a graceful nod of her head to each of them, she smiled and whispered gently, 'Goodbye my guardians; I see that in you I have chosen well.'

The guardians bowed their heads in acknowledgement as the mother goddess disappeared within a shimmer of light. Flitter Trott moved to the diseased branch of alder which lay on the small pile of earth, and smiled as he no longer saw any signs of decay, but the fresh growth of new leaves sprouting from the once dead buds!

Barney and the twins stared at each other in horror. 'There must be *something* we can do,' cried Lorna. 'There just to be a way of tracking them.'

Barney cocked his head to one side as he tried to think of a solution. Suddenly something clicked in his brain, almost like a light switch being turned on. 'Tracking!' he exclaimed. 'Lorna, you said tracking – what about Bouncer? Couldn't he track them for us?'

'I suppose it's worth a try,' Lenny replied thoughtfully, 'after all, he *has* tracked creatures for Flitter Trott hasn't he!'

Lorna nodded in agreement, and climbing down from the bedstead put her arm around Bouncer's neck, taking a gentle grip of the fur as she whispered into his ear, 'Bouncer, find Katie and Rookwort. Go on, boy, track them!'

Bouncer gave her a little growl and carefully began to snuffle around on the ground as he tried to locate

Rookwort and Katie's scent. He moved slowly at first, here and there, allowing Lorna to keep a loose grip of his fur, as Barney and Lenny followed them slowly on the bedstead.

After a few moments Bouncer suddenly gave an excited bark and headed quickly up to the dark entrance which led into the ruins. Lorna and Bouncer quickly jumped back onto the bedstead.

'Well done, Bouncer, you are a clever boy,' said Lorna as she hugged him closely.

'I think that we ought to take it slowly,' muttered Barney. 'Have you still got your dad's torch with you, Lenny?'

'What? Oh sure,' replied Lenny as he pulled out the chrome torch. 'It should be fairly bright,' he added as he switched it on. 'Dad's just put some new batteries in it.'

The beam of the torch lit up the interior of the tunnel as Bouncer suddenly jumped down from the bedstead again and slowly walked ahead of them. 'Bouncer!' cried Barney in panic. 'Where are you going?'

'Don't worry,' Lenny reassured him. 'He's just tracking ahead of us again; aren't you, boy?' Bouncer gave a loud woof then started to quicken his pace a little as he caught the whiff of a stronger scent.

Barney sped up a little as he carefully kept pace with the large grey dog and as quickly as they could, the children made their way deep into the heart of the ancient ruins.

Katie and Rookwort had been walking for a while when they suddenly came upon a very large stone archway. They stopped and, listening carefully, heard howls and hissing coming from somewhere in the distance, and the sound of someone speaking, but couldn't quite make out what the voice was saying.

'I guess that we're here, Katie,' Rookwort whispered.

'What do we do now?' Katie asked nervously.

Rookwort gazed at Katie thoughtfully and muttered to himself, 'I wonder…' after a moment he said, 'Katie, I want you to try something for me.'

Katie looked slightly puzzled, but nodded as Rookwort whispered, 'I want you to concentrate on the Foundling, but using your inner senses. Try to picture her within your mind, and see if you can reach out to her and locate her presence with your feelings. Do you think that you could do that?'

Katie nodded once more. 'I'll try, Uncle, but I'm not sure that I will be able to do it.'

'You must *try*, Katie, for her!' he urged. Katie sighed in submission and stood quite still for a few moments. Then bowing her head she began to visualise the Foundling within her mind. Although she had never actually seen her, she tried to remember the description that Flitter Trott had given her, back at the Goblin Oak.

Slowly she calmed her mind and began to focus on the image of a tiny white badger cub. At first it seemed as if she was trying to look through a thick, many layered curtain, but gradually, little by little, she blocked out all other intruding thoughts and went into an almost trance-like state.

The curtain within her mind began to dissolve slowly, a layer at a time until it finally disappeared. And there she saw it with absolute clarity! A tiny white badger cub, her fur matted with dried blood and covered in filth. Its tiny legs had been cruelly bound together and her breathing had become very shallow.

With her mind Katie reached out to the Foundling, sensing the ever failing beat of its tiny heart. What disturbed Katie the most was that she also sensed the Foundling's fear of its own impending doom.

Realising that there was very little time left, Katie came out of her trance with a shudder, and with tears welling up in her eyes, she collapsed against her uncle's chest.

'Are you alright, Katie?' asked Rookwort, deep concern mirrored in his eyes.

'Oh Uncle,' Katie cried, gulping back the tears. 'She looks so sad and frightened; I think that she's dying!'

The host of black-cloaked figures stood in solemn silence as they gazed up into the night sky. The large hole within the dense mist enabled the Bogwights to observe the alignment of Pangloria's three moons, which would very soon complete the fateful Three Moon Equinox. Here within the Cavern of Doom, the Bogwights had prepared for the coming sacrifice of the Foundling and the leeching of her magic!

In the centre of the dark cavern stood a large altar which had been crudely hewn from a gigantic dead tree stump. Its roots had been cruelly twisted into grotesque looking arms and hands, which gripped the very ground that it sat upon.

The altar had been made by the Bogwights' ancestors who had lived within the ancient fortress many centuries ago, solely for the purpose of carrying out magical sacrifices.

There upon the altar lay the tiny, stricken figure of the Foundling. Her front and hind legs had been cruelly bound together with cords made from dried nettles, her fur had become matted and filthy, and deep furrows had been gouged into her tender skin by cruel claws. She lay there shivering, as she slipped slowly in and out of consciousness, and was now moving closer and closer to death!

Together, at one end of the altar, lay a large dark, crystal flask and a wicked-looking curved knife. Faraak, the Bogwight chieftain, was to act as the high priest of the rite and stood glaring malevolently at his evil brethren. He was only too aware of the need for this rite to succeed. Faraak had always ruled his brethren by fear and by his great strength. But he also knew that he could only rule for as long as he remained stronger than they were. If at any time he failed them he would be overthrown and cast into the Pit of Oblivion, and a new chieftain would be chosen.

The brutal Bogwight chieftain cast a withering look at the brethren once more and hissed, 'My brothers, the fateful time has come for us to fulfil our destiny. The hour of our victory is now at hand, and everything that we have planned and worked for will soon come to pass.'

Howls and hisses of derision filled the air as the Bogwights slobbered and savoured upon the revenge that was soon to come. Faraak nodded to them all in satisfaction as he pointed to the night sky, where they all saw that the three moons were clearly visible. The howls of delight sounded once more as the Bogwights could see that the moons were almost in perfect alignment.

'I will dispatch the Foundling and capture her blood and essence in the Flask of Power; then, my brethren, the magic will be ours,' Faraak drooled in triumph. 'We shall then feast on her flesh in celebration.'

He picked up the cruel curved knife and grasping it

firmly in his clawed hands, raised his arms high, poised ready to deliver the deadly stroke. None of them had noticed the two cloaked figures as they silently entered the cavern!

Bouncer sniffed the air and gave a low growl as he looked from left to right.

'What's the matter, boy?' asked Lorna in a low voice.

'Phew, what a disgusting stench,' Barney moaned, wrinkling up his nose in disgust.

'We must be close to the Bogwights, I reckon,' replied Lenny, retching as his eyes started to water from the effects of the rancid odour.

'Everybody, get your catapults ready and loaded,' ordered Barney in a determined voice. 'I've got a feeling that we're going to have to move fast!'

As if sensing the need for urgency, the bedstead immediately started to pick up speed and hurtled down the tunnel with Bouncer loping ahead towards the archway which led into the Cavern of Doom!

The three moons of Pangloria moved slowly but surely into alignment and at the moment of conjunction, a fiery halo surrounded them, forming the rare but epic Three Moon Equinox.

The night sky suddenly lit up as if daylight had fallen once more on Pangloria. The interior of the immense Cavern of Doom was now bathed in a pale multi-coloured light as Faraak snarled with an evil hiss, 'Now my brethren, now is our time.' He drew back the wicked looking blade in a deadly arc, his lips drawn back into a hideous smile, ready to make the fatal stroke.

Suddenly, a voice shouted tauntingly from somewhere within the depths of the cavern, 'I don't think that you'll have time to deliver that blow, my evil friend,' as a silvery bolt of fiery magic leapt from Rookwort's fingertips, knocking the blade cleanly from the Bogwight's hands.

Faraak was hurled into the air and landed several feet away in a crumpled heap upon the ground. The remaining Bogwights by this time had instantly formed a tight circle around Rookwort and Katie, their eyes greedy in anticipation of revenge at the settling of an old score.

'Ah, old man, we *have* you at last!' they hissed. 'Oh how we have longed for this day, and now we *have* you, *and* your whelp!'

Rookwort and Katie now stood back to back as Rookwort urged Katie in a low voice, 'Remember, Katie, use your magic as you did on the rock earlier, take no chances, and make every strike count!'

Katie nodded as they both went into a crouch, ready to defend themselves from the overwhelming attack that was about to be launched by the Bogwights.

Faraak, meanwhile, unnoticed by Rookwort or Katie, had recovered, and had begun to creep slowly to where the deadly blade lay upon the ground. Picking it up once more, he moved stealthily back to the altar where the Foundling lay.

Faraak stood up slowly and after shaking his head to free it from the pain he was feeling, raised his arms once more, poised and ready to strike. Then with a final roar of triumph, he slashed the curved blade down towards the exposed throat of the Foundling!

The flashing blur of Bouncer's large grey body flew

through the air, his lips drawn back into a terrifying snarl as he crashed into the Bogwights, scattering them like nine pins. Instantly, he rebounded into another giant leap and hurled himself at Faraak, just as the wicked-looking blade slashed down towards the Foundling's exposed throat. He caught the Bogwight chieftain by the back of his neck and promptly tore him to shreds – just in time to prevent the fatal blow from being delivered!

Barney and the twins were now flying around the enormous cavern weaving in and out, and between the Bogwights, carefully aiming their catapults as they flew. Each time one of the Fire-Stones hit its target a Bogwight simply disappeared with a flash and a loud bang!

As Barney landed the bedstead, both he and Lenny leapt down and began to pick off the Bogwights one by one. Lorna had jumped down and immediately ran towards the altar, only to find that her path was barred by two vicious looking Bogwights! They both licked their foul lips hungrily as they made a rush towards her.

'Oh no you don't, that's my *sister*, you foul brutes!' yelled Lenny as he and Barney fired two well-aimed shots at them, and howled with delight as the Bogwights disintegrated with another flash and a loud bang.

'Got you!' shouted Barney, as he looked for his next target.

The scene in the cavern was absolute pandemonium as Katie and Rookwort darted here and there with bolts of magic lancing from their fingers, punishing the attacking Bogwights.

As the battle continued to rage about her, Lorna dashed quickly up to the altar, and stooped to pick up the cruel, curved blade of the sacrificial knife, to cut the nettle ropes which bound the Foundling's legs together.

Very gently she picked up the tiny creature and cradled it in her arms. In a flash, Rookwort was beside her and placed his fingers gently against the Foundling's tiny neck, feeling for a pulse and signs of life.

Meanwhile the battle with the Bogwights continued to rage in the cavern. Bouncer was in his element as he chased them down like rabbits. Each time he caught a Bogwight he simply shredded it with a powerful shake of his head, and the Bogwight being a wraith-like creature, would simply disappear in a puff of smoke!

Barney and Lenny were also in their element as they continued to pour out a deadly hail of Fire-Stones, until they had almost run out of ammunition.

Katie was fearless as she continued to hurl her magic at the Bogwights. Her face was now a mask of hateful fury as she shot bolt after bolt of her magic in revenge for the cruelty that the Bogwights had inflicted upon the Foundling!

Finally, under the relentless onslaught, the Bogwights suddenly gave up! Those who were left were now thoroughly beaten and demoralised. They glided screaming and hissing from the Cavern of Doom.

Finally, now that the battle was over and there were no Bogwights left to fight, Barney, Katie and Lenny rushed over to Lorna and Rookwort.

Upon seeing the Foundling cradled in Lorna's arms, Katie bit her lip and asked, 'Is she still alive?'

'Yes,' replied Rookwort sadly, 'But only *just*, I'm afraid – though I'll try to do what I can for her, for now at least.'

He reached into a pocket of his tunic and brought out the brown leather flask of Spring Mead. He pulled out the stopper and very gently poured a tiny amount into the Foundling's mouth.

After a few moments the tiny albino cub licked its parched lips slowly. 'Oh look,' cried Lorna softly. 'She's lapping, do you think that it might make her well again?'

'I doubt it – but it should give her enough strength, I think, to get her to a friend of mine. She will be able to heal her,' Rookwort replied gently. 'But we will have to move quickly.'

Staring at the children, Rookwort suddenly experienced a feeling of great pride and said, 'You've all done extremely well and I'm immensely proud of you. You certainly didn't waste time on those Bogwights, did you? And old Bouncer here, well, if it hadn't been for *him*, we would have been too late!'

He paused for a moment and then added urgently, 'Barney! I need you to fly your bed-scapator faster than you have ever flown it before, and you are going to have to take us to the *one* person that I know who can heal the Foundling. Can you do that?'

'You bet I can! Just show me the way,' he replied, already making his way to the bedstead.

Within seconds everyone had climbed aboard and Barney took the bedstead up through the large hole in the roof of the cavern, climbing high above the Rotten Marshes.

Rookwort took out his Pointer and said, 'Show me the way to the Enchanted Forest.' The Pointer spun and pointed northwards, and Barney headed in that direction.

It was almost as if the bedstead had sensed the urgent need for speed, and they were now flying faster than Barney had ever flown before; as the ground below them appeared to be just a blur. The Foundling still lay curled up in Lorna's arms and seemed to be sleeping and breathing more easily, mainly due to the effects of Rookwort's Spring Mead.

Katie became very quiet and thoughtful after the battle with the Bogwights. Occasionally she would glance at her uncle and it seemed that she was going to ask him a question, but her uncle, as though he had sensed it, would lean over and speak to Barney about their direction, almost as though he was trying to avoid having to speak to her.

Although they flew for many miles, it seemed like no time at all when they came to the borders of a very large forest. The first light of dawn had arrived and Rookwort asked Barney to bring the bed-scapator down below the level of the tree tops.

They flew more slowly now and the bed-scapator weaved its way in and out of the trees as it headed deeper and deeper into the heart of the woodland.

The forest itself was very much like Badger Wood but far denser and considerably larger. Rookwort explained to them that this too, was also a haven, and contained its own Foundling. It was from one of the guardians of this haven that he was now seeking help.

After travelling many miles into the Enchanted Forest, they came upon a clearing within a dense canopy of trees. Rookwort instructed Barney to land in the middle of the clearing and they all dismounted and stood, quietly waiting.

'Why have we stopped here, Uncle?' asked Katie.

'We're waiting for someone,' Rookwort replied with a smile.

'They will probably know that we are here by now and will be along shortly I should think.'

Rookwort's instinct had proved right, and before

long a tiny waif-like figure stepped into the clearing. Everyone stared in disbelief at what they saw – a small childlike figure of a young girl, who in return gazed back at them all inquisitively.

The girl who stood before them had hair that was almost white in colour. From the middle of her shoulders sprouted a pair of large, gossamer-like wings, and she wore clothes that were exquisitely made from a translucent silky material, which looked like real flowers.

The children continued to stare at her in wonder as the tiny figure stepped closer giving them all a serene smile. Rookwort turned to the children and with his usual mocking smile announced, 'This, my young friends, is a creature of the faerie world! Yes,' he added with a nod as he noted the look of surprise registered in their faces, 'faeries really do exist!'

~ CHAPTER ELEVEN ~

Izzy Dewdrop

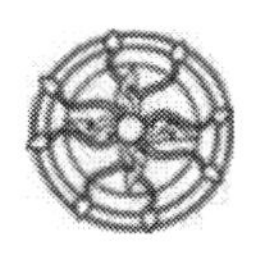

The faerie creature smiled as she greeted them all. 'Hello, Rook, my old friend; what brings you so far from home? Could it be that you no longer wish to live apart from other living creatures?' She waved in the direction of the children and added, 'I see that you have also gained some new friends.'

The girl stopped suddenly and craning her tiny neck to look, she asked Lorna, 'What is it that you have in your arms, child? I sense an aura of innate magic about it.'

'All in good time, Izzy,' Rookwort answered. 'I fear that we have an interesting tale to tell you.' He then turned to the children and with a graceful wave of his hand said, 'Please allow me to introduce you to Izzy Dewdrop, a creature of the faerie world and a guardian of this haven.'

Rookwort introduced each one of the children and Izzy Dewdrop smiled and waved a greeting to each of them in turn. Bouncer casually trotted up to Izzy, sniffing at her as though he were checking her out, and promptly lay down on the grass, allowed the faerie creature to climb up onto his neck and stroke his ears, crooning softly as she did so.

'I see that you all have a tale to tell, *that* much is obvious. So I shall just sit here patiently, with this very intelligent dog, and hear your story without any interruptions,' Izzy added, as she headed off a remark that Lenny was about to make regarding Bouncer and his love of fleas!

Rookwort wasted no time and gave Izzy the details of their adventure and told her everything that had occurred regarding the taking of the Foundling by the Bogwights, and its effects upon Badger Wood.

He also explained about the children and where they were all from. When he mentioned Ezekiel, the Maiden and Flitter Trott, he saw the hint of surprise mirrored in Izzy's eyes but more so, the strange glance that she gave Katie when he mentioned that she was related to both Ezekiel and himself.

It had taken the best part of an hour to tell Izzy everything, and he ended his tale by saying, 'There you have it! Now you know *all* that there is to know. Can you do anything for the Foundling? She desperately needs your help and I do not have the skills to heal her hurts completely.'

Izzy leapt nimbly off Bouncer's neck and moved towards Lorna and the Foundling. She placed a tiny hand upon the Foundling's head, and closing her eyes she used her woodland magic to probe deeply for the nature of the injuries that the Foundling had suffered.

With a look of deep concern reflected in her eyes, she turned to Rookwort and replied sadly, 'I will do all that I can for her, Rook, but she has suffered many serious hurts at the hands of the Bogwights. They care nothing for any living creature, and have treated her most cruelly.

'What I also perceive, however, is that you have not told me all that there is to know. Izzy gave Katie a searching glance and turning back to Rookwort added, 'I believe that you are holding something back something concerning this child – something perhaps – that you do not yet fully understand.'

Izzy stared deeply into Rookwort's eyes and said with a sigh, 'But now is not the time, we must do what we can for this poor creature. You will all need to come back to my bower, there I have powders and roots which will make her strong and woodland magic to heal her hurts.'

They all climbed aboard the bedstead once more as Izzy flew on before them, with Barney always keeping her in sight as he followed her deeper into the Enchanted Forest.

They came at last to a grove of very large trees – these were certainly the tallest trees that any of the children had ever seen before! In the centre of the grove stood a large, gnarled old oak tree, and nearby they spotted a ring of what appeared to be very large mushrooms and toadstools. This, Rookwort informed them, was a faerie ring, a meeting place for the wood-folk of the faerie world.

Izzy had disappeared into the bowels of the old oak tree, and while she was away, Rookwort delved into one of the pockets of his tunic and brought out two round loaves of bread, a large chunk of delicious-looking cheese, butter, and a large flask of ale. From another pocket he produced wooden plates, cups, and knives for them all. He even managed to conjure up a large, tasty biscuit for Bouncer, who wagged his tail in excitement at the thought of such a treat.

They were soon chomping away ravenously at the feast set before them. It was certainly the most enjoyable picnic in the sun that the children had ever had and they quickly demolished the whole fare and lay contentedly on the grass awaiting Izzy's return.

Lorna kept a regular check on the Foundling, who appeared to be sleeping soundly, and in the warmth of the morning sunshine they all began to feel a pleasant drowsiness creeping up on them. Barney was in a sort of half sleep when he thought he heard a soft, but high pitched hum. He looked around him lazily trying to discover the source of the strange noise.

Sitting on the mushrooms and toadstools, were a number of faerie-like creatures. Some were flying, others running here and there as they chattered excitedly in their musical voices.

One had decided to perch herself upon Bouncer's large black nose, and was crooning softly to him as he tried to focus on her which made him appear very cross-eyed!

Barney roused the others and they all took great delight at the antics of the adorable wood-folk, as they danced and cavorted around the beautiful forest glade. Rookwort smiled at the children and said, 'It appears that we are witnessing a rare faerie gathering.'

Suddenly, flying into their midst and landing gently within the centre of the faerie ring came Izzy Dewdrop, who called for silence and began to explain, in faerie tongue of course, about the plight of the Foundling from Badger Wood.

She informed her brothers and sisters about the defeat of the Bogwights and revealed how their evil plans to dominate Pangloria and other worlds had been thwarted by Barney and his friends. The faerie gathering smiled at Rookwort and the children then gave them all a polite, round of applause.

Izzy turned to Rookwort and the children and thanked them all. 'It appears that we have much to be grateful for. We have always regarded you as our friend, Rookwort, but doubly so from this moment forth.' She looked at each of the children in turn and added, 'You too are our special friends and even though you *are* from another world, you will be forever welcome to come and stay in our realm.'

She went over to the Foundling and calling for her brothers and sisters to join her, she turned once again to Rookwort and announced, 'But now it is a time for the healing to begin.'

Izzy then beckoned the wood-folk to form a circle around the Foundling, and they all placed their tiny hands on the body of the tiny white badger cub. After several long moments of complete silence a haunting, musical sound filled the forest glade, which slowly built up into a crescendo!

It soared and spread to the very depths of the forest as every faerie, sprite, brownie and woodland creature sang their bird-like song. As the sunlight blazed through the canopy of the trees, the children and Rookwort felt their spirits suddenly lifted by the haunting melody of the tiny wood-folk, such was the power of their magic. Quite suddenly the Foundling raised her head and began to mew gently in response. Izzy held out a tiny, sparkling crystal bottle and began to trickle a clear liquid between the Foundling's lips.

She lapped at the liquid gratefully and almost instantly rolled onto her paws and stood up. The Foundling began to move, stiffly at first, slowly wandering around the faerie ring and suddenly started to move faster, as she playfully cavorted around the tiny wood-folk, happy to be alive and safe once more.

'Almost the end of a successful adventure, I think,' Rookwort smiled, as Barney, Katie, and the twins moved over to play with the tiny little badger cub who was now chasing Bouncer around rather boisterously.

Lorna stooped down and gently picked up the Foundling and held it to her chest. There were tears in both Katie and Lorna's eyes as they began to cuddle the tiny creature, as she began to lick them in return, almost as if she was thanking them.

Izzy Dewdrop gazed up at Rookwort as he held her tiny figure on his hand and whispered, 'Perhaps now, my old friend, you will not lead such a lonely existence?'

'No – I don't expect that I will,' he replied quietly.

'You will of course have to confide your suspicions to Katie,' Izzy advised him seriously, 'but you know that already don't you?'

'Yes, I do,' Rookwort answered, 'but I think that it's best if she asks Ezekiel first, because I'm not sure that even *I* know the whole story yet.'

'Yes, perhaps it is.' Izzy agreed. 'I see much of her grandmother in her and her grandfather too,' and she stroked Rookwort's cheek gently with her tiny hand, as she added, 'I knew right away of course, as soon as I saw her, after all it is the gift that my race are privileged to possess.'

'The Seer, Amarelda, she also knew,' Rookwort,

admitted ruefully, as he smiled at Izzy.

'Yes, she too would have sensed it of course,' Izzy replied. 'Amarelda has a rare gift – when you consider that she is a human.' Izzy smiled understandingly at Rookwort and as she jumped gently from his hand she whispered, 'It's time for you all to leave, for now, and get your Foundling back to where she belongs and is needed.'

~ CHAPTER TWELVE ~

Home Again

Rookwort and the children waved farewell to Izzy Dewdrop and the group of tiny wood-folk who were standing around the faerie ring.

With great sadness at leaving their new found friends they climbed back up onto the bed-scapator ready for the journey back to the Valley of the Fiery Holes. The children gazed around them in wonder, still not quite believing that they were actually in the realm of faeries. But they were learning quickly however that nothing should ever really surprise them, especially in the magical world of Pangloria!

As they were about to leave, Izzy flew onto Barney's shoulder and whispered into his ear, 'Now that you have the means of travelling between our worlds, we shall expect to see you all again soon! Do not forget us,

Barney. We have a lot of things in common and many adventures to share. Always remember that.'

She then turned to Katie, and looking deeply into her eyes, she gave her some good advice, 'My child, I know that you are confused and feel that you have been ill used, but you will not always feel this way. Do not blame your uncle, for he is as much a plaything of fate as we all are. Have a good long talk to your uncle Ezekiel when you get home and persuade him to give you the answers to those burning questions that lie within your heart. You have an aura of powerful white magic about you. I know this to be so because I can sense it – and my senses are never wrong!'

Izzy Dewdrop turned and spoke to the twins, wishing them a safe journey home and inviting them to return with Barney and Katie, and after embracing Bouncer and the Foundling one final time, she thanked everyone for their bravery and said, 'Goodbye, my friends. Keep yourselves safe and return to us soon.'

They all waved goodbye a final time, as Barney commanded the bed-scapator to take them to the Valley of the Fiery Holes.

In an instant Barney's bed shot up into the sky, until it was high above the clouds, and stopping momentarily, it found its correct heading and then flew like the wind, making its way towards Rookwort's home.

After what seemed like only minutes, although they had in fact travelled a very long way, they found themselves flying high up, over the Wormwood Wastes. The Stag Mountains came quickly into view, as Barney began to guide the bedstead around in a wide spiralling arc, descending gradually until at last they could see the

Rotten Marshes far below.

The marshes were cloaked in a thick, dense mist, which appeared to be as brooding and inhospitable as ever. Barney held his course for a while and before long they had entered the Valley of the Fiery Holes, where Barney landed the bed-scapator close to Rookwort's cabin.

They climbed down from the bedstead and trooped into the cabin which, as always, was warm and welcoming. Soon they were all sitting happily and comfortably drinking mugs of hot sweet tea and munching on hunks of crusty bread and a whole round of creamy cheese.

The Foundling and Bouncer lay snuggled up together cosy and warm next to Rookwort's roaring fire, both of them snoring gently. Lenny, Lorna and Barney were busily involved in a heated debate regarding the finer points of shooting Fire-Stones from their catapults, as Katie looked on, highly amused at their banter.

'Well of course it's all in the grip you know,' Lenny stated pompously, 'and I ought to know, seeing as I popped the greatest number of Bogwights!' he added giving Rookwort and Katie a sly wink.

'Says who?' cried Barney and Lorna together.

Then, spotting the twitch of a mocking smile beginning to appear on her brother's lips, Lorna laughed and said, 'You know what, Barney, he's winding us up again.'

'And succeeding,' Katie chipped in with a snort of laughter.

Rookwort simply shook his head and drank deeply from a large mug of ale, then wiping his lips on the sleeve of his tunic, he announced loudly, 'Well, as sad as it may be, I do think it's about time that you all headed back home. If I know Flitter Trott he'll be really fretting about the Foundling by now.'

Barney and the twins started to protest, but Rookwort held up his hands, as though he was fending off an attack and replied, 'Whoa! I know that you don't want to return just yet but you've got to get back sometime! And it's not as if you aren't *ever* coming back again, now is it?'

'Are you certain that you really want me to return, Uncle?' Katie asked sharply, and immediately regretted the question, as she saw the expression of hurt, reflected in her uncle's face.

'Katie, of course I want you to come back,' he sighed wearily, with tears in his eyes. 'But I want you to do something for me. When you get back home, I want you to speak to Ezekiel and get him to give you the answers to some of those questions that you have. I can't answer them for you, because I'm still not sure what I make of it all, but ask him for me. Put him on the spot and get him to explain.'

Katie looked at her uncle and nodded tearfully, and stepping forward she fell into his arms. The old man hugged her tightly, patting her back gently as she replied, 'Oh Uncle Rook, of course I will, and I'll be back soon, just you wait and see. Mind you, that's only if Barney will give me a lift,' she added with a tearful laugh.

Barney smiled and nodded his head in agreement, as Lenny quipped, 'Yeah that goes for all of us, why should Katie and Barney have all the fun?'

Rookwort laughed out loud as he replied, 'And I'll be very glad to have you all here. After all, you've made an old man feel quite young again.'

After bidding Rookwort farewell, for the present, they climbed onto the bedstead and all nodded as he shouted, 'Pass my regards on to that brother of mine, Katie – and don't forget to come back!'

Then with a final wave, Barney shouted loudly, 'Bed! Please take us back to Badger Wood!'

With a lurch the bedstead shot like a rocket, high into the sky, and as they all looked back they saw that Rookwort appeared as no more than a tiny speck on the ground. The bedstead stopped in mid-air for a split second, and in a graceful arc made its way towards Flahgens Peake.

As they approached the mountain they rose higher and higher above its snow covered peak. Like a climbing roller coaster the bedstead reached the top of its arc and suddenly plummeted into a steep dive towards the side of the mountain.

The girls both screamed at the top of their voices and Bouncer howled as the bedstead crashed into the mountain side. For a split second they were engulfed by the now familiar whooshing sound and suddenly found themselves back within Badger Wood, flying in a large circle around the Mound.

As they stared down into the depths of the wood they spotted the tiny figure of Flitter Trott peering up at them anxiously as he waited for them to land.

Barney landed in a small clearing fairly close to the Goblin Oak, and as Flitter Trott ran up to them he cried impatiently, 'Well? Did you do it? Did you manage to rescue her?'

They climbed down from the bedstead and smiled as Lenny gave the wood sprite a jubilant 'thumbs up'. Flitter Trott stepped forward and peered at the Foundling who was nestling fast asleep in Katie's arms.

'She *is* okay isn't she?' he asked worriedly. 'I mean, she's not sick or anything?'

'No she's fine, Flit,' Katie assured him. 'Izzy Dewdrop and the wood-folk of the Enchanted Forest healed her.'

'Did they really! Well, how about that?' He chuckled. 'You rescuing her *and* meeting one of my sisters. Who would have thought it? I was born in the Enchanted Forest, you know. But that's another story for another time,' he added, with a wistful look in his eyes.

He turned to Barney and asked, 'Could we have the use of your bed-scapator once more? It's only a short journey this time – I need to go to the Foundling's sett.' He paused, noting the puzzled look on their faces. 'She has to be returned to the creatures of the wood right away, you see.' Turning to the others he said, 'I only need Barney and myself to do this. The wild creatures of the wood are very shy and tend to hide from man. They would feel, well, threatened by your presence and I know that you would never do them any harm, but they have been through such a lot recently, and a group of children might scare them. You know how it is?'

As he gazed at Lorna, Flitter Trott could see the sadness reflected in her eyes as she replied, 'Of course we understand, Flit.' Both Katie and Lenny nodded their heads in silent agreement, as Lorna asked, 'Can we say goodbye to her, one last time?'

Flitter Trott smiled sadly, as the three children stroked the Foundling's head gently. Both Lorna and Katie kissed her lightly on her brow, and the Foundling opened its tiny eyes, staring at them sadly for a moment as if acknowledging them all, then after licking their hands gently she closed her eyes once more.

Barney and Flitter Trott climbed onto the bedstead, the Foundling cradled gently in the sprite's arms. 'We'll only be a few minutes,' he whispered. 'We'll meet you back at the Goblin Oak – it lies just beyond that large willow tree behind you.'

Katie and the twins nodded and after waving goodbye to the Foundling a final time, turned and headed towards the willow tree.

Barney and Flitter Trott flew across Dingle Brook, into the deepest part of Badger Wood and landed gently in a tiny clearing which was just about large enough to accommodate the bedstead.

They climbed down and began to walk silently into the wood. After walking a short distance they came upon a small sandy covered clearing, where they could see the entrance to the badgers' sett.

Flitter Trott moved forward quietly, the Foundling still cradled in his arms as Barney kept himself hidden within the bushes at a safe distance. He watched closely as Flitter Trott gently laid the Foundling at the entrance of the sett and heard him call out gently to the small family of badgers who were settled deep within.

As Flitter Trott moved back to join Barney they saw the large family of badgers slowly emerge one by one from the entrance of the sett. Each badger began to sniff at the Foundling and joyfully began to lick her fur, covering her with their scent which roused the tiny cub from her slumber. They could hear the Foundling whimpering in happiness and heard the mewing of her siblings as they greeted her one by one.

The Foundling finally turned to Barney and Flitter Trott, giving them one last look of gratitude, and then walked slowly into the sett followed by her family.

Almost immediately they felt a warm summer breeze sweep gently through the wood. And as they gazed upwards to the sky they were astonished to see the dark ominous clouds that had hung over Badger Wood for several days suddenly disappear as if by magic!

'Well,' said Flitter Trott with a sigh, 'she's back where she belongs, safe and sound. Now the wood can continue to survive peacefully as it always has done.'

Barney felt the keen bite of bittersweet emotions – sad, but at the same time happy that things had turned out for the best. 'Come on, Flit,' he said suddenly, with a grin, 'I'll race you back to Goblin Oak!'

'You've got *no* chance!' Flitter Trott replied with a grin, 'I'll have a pot of tea made by the time *you* get there.'

Flitter Trott was right! By the time that Barney had gotten to the gigantic oak tree everyone was drinking tea and tucking in to a plateful of large jam tarts. As they were munching away merrily Flitter Trott gave Katie a sly sideways glance and asked what she thought of her uncle Rook.

Katie told him about her visit to see the Seer, Amarelda, and of her conversation with Izzy Dewdrop. She also told him about the magic she had used in the Bogwights lair and how Rookwort had helped her to discover her hidden powers. 'I always suspected that there was something odd about me, Flit,' she confessed, 'but I've always been afraid to ask.'

Flitter Trott moved towards Katie, clasping her hands between his own; staring up into her eyes he replied, 'Katie Crabtree! I could answer *all* of your questions and put your mind at ease – right now! But it isn't my place to do so. You *must* persuade Ezekiel to give you the answers. Only *you* can do this, do you understand?'

'I know, Flit, and I will ask him,' Katie promised.

Smiling, Flitter Trott whispered, 'Good.' Then he suddenly jumped up and added, 'Oh, by the way – we had a spot of trouble from that young man who's been hunting our pheasants and rabbits while you were away.'

'Who? Jed Hopwood? What's he done now?' demanded Lenny.

'He decided to come into the wood again with two friends of his this time, and set a number of cruel metal traps,' Flitter Trott, replied. 'But the Maiden and I soon sorted them out, *and* their wicked traps. I don't think they'll try that again in a hurry.' Flitter Trott then went on to tell them about how Jed and his friends had fled from the wood – all battered and bruised.

The children roared with laughter at the thought of Jed nursing a possible broken ankle! 'Well it jolly well serves them right! The cruel beasts,' cried Lorna angrily. And of course, as a guardian of Badger Wood, Flitter Trott had agreed with the Maiden and Ezekiel that they would never breathe a word to another living soul about their part in the magical rite that had taken place the previous evening. It was something that would only remain a secret between the three of them, so Flitter Trott made no mention of it to the children.

After chatting for a while longer the children decided to head off to their homes, and climbing aboard the bedstead once more, *and* after promising to visit him the next day, they waved goodbye to Flitter Trott.

Barney then ordered the bedstead to take him home. Almost immediately the bedstead gave a lurch, and sped quickly through Badger Wood. Before they knew it, they found themselves back once more within Barney's bedroom.

'Have we been dreaming or did we really have an adventure?' the twins wondered, looking somewhat puzzled.

'Oh it's been quite real I can assure you,' Barney replied.

'Barney, don't you think that you'd better change back into your pyjamas, before your mum gets back?' Katie asked. 'You're supposed to be ill, *remember*!'

'Oh crumbs – I'd forgotten all about that,' Barney grinned. 'Look, just turn your heads a moment, will you?'

Katie and the twins peered out of Barney's bedroom window, as they heard the rustling sound of Barney changing clothes.

The children sat on Barney's bedstead for over an hour chatting and laughing about their amazing adventure, still not quite believing that it had actually happened at all.

In what appeared to no time at all they heard the sound of the front door of the cottage opening and closing, and Barney's mum bustling up the stairs.

The bedroom door opened and in walked Olivia, looking red faced and out of breath, 'My goodness,' she exclaimed breathlessly. 'That seemed to take forever. How are you feeling, dear? Your friends haven't been tiring you out I hope?'

There was a sudden burst of laughter from the children and Olivia seemed quite perplexed as she asked, 'What's the matter? Did I say something funny?'

'No, Mum,' Barney answered, with tears of mirth rolling down his cheeks. 'It's just a joke between us, that's all.'

'Well, it's good to see that you're on the mend,' Olivia commented, 'but I *do* think it's time that you had a little peace and quiet, my lad – so say goodbye to your friends for now, and you can see them again tomorrow, if you're well enough that is.'

Lorna looked at Barney's mum and said, 'Thanks for letting us come up to see Barney, Mrs Betts, he *really* did need cheering up.'

'Well that's very kind of you, my dear, very kind indeed,' replied Barney's mum with a smile, and she caught herself thinking, *what a charming girl, oh I do wish I had a daughter…*

'Well, I'll be off now, Barney,' said Katie, giving Barney a sly smile. 'I have a few things to discuss with Uncle Ezekiel, so I'll see you all tomorrow.'

Following Katie's lead, Lorna added, 'We had better be going as well, Barney – we promised to help Dad in the garden.' They followed Olivia through Barney's bedroom door and Lenny paused to call Bouncer, who gave Barney a loud bark as he followed Lenny out of the bedroom.

Barney lay back onto his pillow with both hands behind his head, gave a low whistle and simply said, 'Brilliant!'

ACKNOWLEDGEMENTS

Many thanks to author Debbie Young for reading this, my first book and offering me very sound advice, and to the eagle-eyed Helen Baggott for her editing services and advice. Bless you both.

A message from the author

Thank you for reading this book. If you enjoyed the story, keep your eyes open for book number two in the Tales of Pangloria series *Beyond the Maelstrom*, due to be published shortly.

16027588R00106

Printed in Great Britain
by Amazon